TRUE L♥VE, THE SPHINX,
and Other Unsolvable Riddles

Also by Tyne O'Connell

The Calypso Chronicles:
Pulling Princes
Stealing Princes
Dueling Princes
Dumping Princes

TRUE LOVE, THE SPHINX,
and Other Unsolvable Riddles

♥ ♥ ♥   *A Comedy in Four Voices*   ♥ ♥ ♥

TYNE O'CONNELL

BLOOMSBURY

Published by Bloomsbury U.S.A. Children's Books
175 Fifth Avenue, New York, NY 10010
Distributed to the trade by Holtzbrinck Publishers

Library of Congress Cataloging-in-Publication Data
O'Connell, Tyne.
True love, the sphinx, and other unsolvable riddles: a comedy in four voices /
by Tyne O'Connell. — 1st U.S. ed.
p.   cm.
Summary: While on a class trip in Egypt, two teenaged best friends from an American
private boys' school and two teenaged best friends from a British private girls' school
meet each other, and must endure many misunderstandings on their path to true love.
ISBN-13: 978-1-59990-050-6 • ISBN-10: 1-59990-050-5
[1. School field trips—Fiction.   2. Love—Fiction.   3. Best friends—Fiction.
4. Egypt—Fiction.]   I. Title.
PZ7.O2168Tr2007   [Fic]—dc22   2007002596

First U.S. Edition 2007
Typeset by Westchester Book Composition
Printed in the U.S.A. by Quebecor World Fairfield
2   4   6   8   10   9   7   5   3   1

All papers used by Bloomsbury U.S.A. are natural, recyclable products
made from wood grown in well-managed forests. The manufacturing processes
conform to the environmental regulations of the country of origin.

Dedicated to Zad, Cordelia, and Katia for being inspirational, but most of all, for being the extraordinary creatures they are!

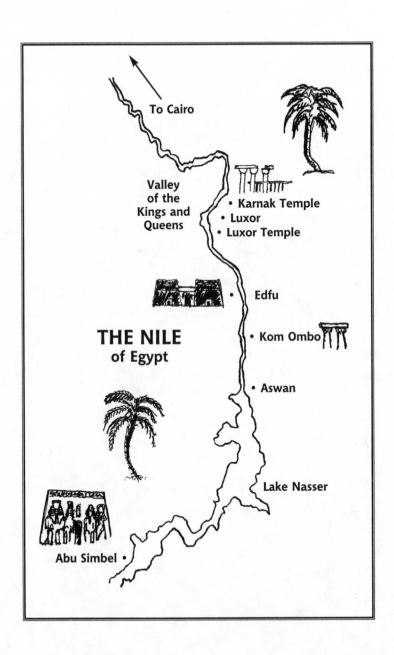

To Cairo

Valley
of the
Kings and
Queens

• Karnak Temple
• Luxor
• Luxor Temple

• Edfu

THE NILE
of Egypt

• Kom Ombo

• Aswan

Lake Nasser

Abu Simbel •

The riddle of the Sphinx:

What walks on four legs in the morning, two legs at noon, and three legs in the evening?

CHAPTER 1

··· SAM ···

February, Bowers School for Boys, Manhattan

I figured there must be more to life than girls. I just wasn't that interested in letting people know that I cared.

Most of the guys in geography class that afternoon were e-mailing, texting, or fooling around on their BlackBerrys and iPods. After Carol wrote the word *Egypt* on the whiteboard, I started to check out the new lens for my Leica. I like to think of myself as a man-of-the-moment sort of guy, and I'd been waiting for this particular lens for weeks.

After unpacking, I scanned the instructions and began attaching it to my camera. It wasn't like I was going to miss out on any great chunk of wisdom. No one actually thinks geography is a real subject any more than Carol's a real teacher. Don't get me wrong, we all kind of like her, but she's totally off the wall—and at Bowers that's saying something!

Take Professor Ali. He spent an entire term dementedly slapping the board with a whiteboard eraser and occasionally slinging it at boys he was convinced were "out to get him." Our headmaster finally wrote a letter to parents regretfully announcing that Professor Ali was taking time off for a sabbatical. I mean, how dumb do they think people are? Even parents know that "sabbatical" is code for looney bin.

I looked up at Carol again in case she was writing something relevant, but no, she was drawing a map, oblivious to the fact that no one, not even Yo, the Official School Geek, was paying any attention. Yo was wearing his virtual reality visor and moving his limbs robotically. Yo is one of my closest friends. His real name is Thomas, but when he first came to Bowers, he had been playing up his African American roots and said "yo" all the time. So we all started calling him "Yo" so we could say, "yo, Yo!" It had seemed funny at the time.

Carol turned around and asked whimsically, "Don't you love the romance of the desert, boys?"

We all laughed. Seriously, we thought she was joking. She wasn't.

She scowled. "You are the most immature and emotionally lost class in this school."

We were a patient bunch, but even for us it was too much to be classified as immature and emotionally lost by Carol: a middle-aged woman in a tie-dyed hippy skirt, who regularly lost control. On her first day she "invited" us to call her by her first name and to think of her as a unique and mystical being "much like your-selves."

Calling teachers by their first names was against school policy. I suspect thinking of them as unique and mystical beings was too, but what can you do? The first time one of us didn't call her Carol, she went postal.

Another one of my closest friends, Astin, says school is like a war and we're foot soldiers. That's why he has a crew cut. He says the only way to deal is to keep your head down, get good grades, and count yourself lucky if you get out alive. If Astin gets out, I have a suspicion that he'll become a James Bond character. Even though he's not British, he's got that whole suave thing going on. Also, he can raise one eyebrow, which the girls love.

Speaking of the fairer sex, I sent a text, suggesting cof-fee after school to this Spence girl I'd chosen as my weekly focus. Holly had asked me to get her on the invite list to my mother's fashion show. I figured that meant she wanted to hook up. She was the usual straight-off-the-conveyer-belt fashionista I meet all the time. They're all identical, equipped with long blond hair and perfect figures.

My very best friend, Salah, hates the conveyor-belt girls I date, but if you ask me—which he never does—he's got an unrealistic set of standards that can lead only to disappointment. Luckily for me, Salah is considered one of the most eligible teenagers in Manhattan, and his indifference to most girls has driven a legion of cuties into my less discerning arms. I try not to care that I may be their second-best option.

Carol was still off in her own world, decorating her map with details of palm trees and monuments. Seriously, our parents paid good money for her to doodle on a whiteboard. Give me a break.

I threw a piece of Styrofoam from the lens at Salah, who was two chairs in front, only it hit Yo on his VR visor. He turned around, removed the visor, and gave me his trademark withering look. That withering look will make him a lot of money one day when he's working for Morgan Stanley.

"Who can tell me what continent Egypt is part of?" Carol asked.

I flicked another piece at Salah. This one hit its mark with a satisfying *thwack*, and a few guys, including Yo, laughed. Salah turned around, prearmed with rubber bands on each thumb and forefinger, pistol-style, which he fired in my direction. I used my BlackBerry as an effective block, but Carol was not impressed.

"Yes, very funny," she said with a surprising amount of venom for a unique, mystical being. "Now if you can act your age for a moment, perhaps you can tell me which countries Egypt shares a border with?"

No one said anything. Passive aggression was the only weapon we held, and we weren't afraid to use it.

"No one? The so-called best of the best of your generation and you've managed to remain oblivious to one of the world's greatest civilizations?"

Sarcasm is such a lame weapon for a teacher.

I went back to my camera until I was interrupted by the shrill cries of Carol calling my name.

"Sam?"

I looked up from the new lens. "Yes, Carol?"

"What do you know about Egypt, Sam?"

"Egypt?" I repeated, stalling for time.

"Yes, Egypt!"

"Well, it's a country. More or less triangular in shape"—I pointed to the map she'd drawn—"and there's a sort of line that runs down the middle."

"A *river*, Sam. It's called a *river*," she snapped.

"Yeah, that's what I said, a river running down the middle."

Carol's lips formed a tight little angry line. "Very clever. What else? What is Egypt famous for. Anyone?"

Great—I was off the hook. I made a few adjustments to the lens. The only thing I feel more passionately about than girls is photography, and getting a new lens is like hooking up with a new girl. Sometimes the lens stayed in my life longer than a girl, but more often than not a new lens turned into just another gadget I'd tire of in a week. But I will never fall out of love with my 1954 Leica M series. It was the first bayonet-style inter-changeable lens camera advertised as "a lifetime invest-ment in perfect photography."

My dad bought me one of the original Leica posters at an auction. And the camera used to be his when he was a photographer. That was before he ran off with some French model to live in San Tropez. For the last three years my dad and I have only spoken on the phone. It's kind of weird because I can tell when we talk that he thinks we still have the same really close bond we had when he was at home. He doesn't seem aware that all we ever talk about is photography. For instance, he doesn't even know I broke my arm—in an embarrass-ing fall from a curb on the way home from school. He also doesn't know that my mom depends on me for emotional support she should have been getting from him. Like there was this time she broke up with some loser and I had to stay home and watch sad movies with her for three weeks. My girlfriend ended up dumping me over it. During that period I couldn't hang out, Salah came over a lot. We ate popcorn and he dissed all the guys in the sad movies, which made my mom laugh. She's got some pretty cool guy at the moment. I hope it lasts because when she's in love, she never asks where I'm going or what I'm doing.

My love for my cameras is unnatural according to

Salah. He might be right. I suspect my passion for my Hasselblad H2 might be verging on a mania. I couldn't live without my Hass. It does about everything a guy could wish for in a camera—if only it could manage my relationships with girls.

I was startled out of camera heaven by Carol. "What is Egypt most famous for?" she was yelling again.

I looked around but everyone was just doing his own thing, completely not interested in her or me or what Egypt was famous for. While I adjusted my camera, I worked out that Carol probably wanted me to give her an answer like "the pyramids" or "the sphinx." But I wasn't going to give her the satisfaction. Finally, I looked up and said, "Salah?" My face was totally deadpan—he is Egyptian after all.

The face that had disappointed half of the female population of the Upper East Side and was this month gracing the cover of some socialite magazine, turned around. "What was that, Sam?"

Carol was thrilled. "Of course, Salah. What can you tell us about your people?"

Salah didn't bother to turn back to Carol. He just kept right on looking at me, a grin plastered across his handsome features.

I used my chin to direct Salah's attention back to Carol. "Carol wants to know about your people, man."

He spun around to face Carol. "My bros, you mean,

Carol? My bloods?" He was good. He didn't even sound sarcastic.

"Yes, what can you tell us about them?"

"We're a good-looking, intelligent people, Carol. Great heads for business and bodies for—"

"Oh, Salah! I would have thought that *you* of all people would take Egypt seriously!"

Salah turned back to me, clearly baffled. "What is she talking about?"

"Egypt!" Carol snapped, stomping a Birkenstock in fury. "I'm talking about Egypt!"

Salah gestured for her to calm down. "Okay, Carol, chill. Don't forget, you are a mystical and unique being."

This seemed to mollify her. "Thank you, Salah."

"Kind of like us Egyptians," he added.

I truly believe that Salah is one of those rare people who is entirely oblivious to the power of his quiet charm. But his oblivion didn't change the fact that he had the world at his feet. He had no guile, no agenda. When someone wants nothing from you, it makes them very relaxing to be around. Everyone felt easy with Salah because all he ever wanted was a good time. His family was insanely wealthy even by Bowers standards, yet he's got this whole antimaterialism thing going on, which on anyone else wouldn't sit comfortably with such insane wealth. Like, even though his house is opulently decorated, his own room is totally simple. A desk, a Mac, and a Futon covered in pillows. His one nod to wealth was his love of the suits he has tailor-made in London every year—only he said they were better than tailor-made. They were "bespoke"—whatever that is. He teams them with no-name accessories—the cheapest sneakers, Wal-Mart shirts or tees. And yet every year, he is declared the best-dressed teenager in our school. He could easily be the sort of guy I hated if it weren't for the fact that he's also easier to talk to than anyone I know. Also he's got too much on me now for us *not* to be friends.

I can tell Salah things that it would kill me to admit to anyone else. For example, Salah is the only one of my friends who would ever get that I don't just want to be the next big thing in fashion photography. Spending my life taking photographs of hot models might be a dream job for lots of my friends, but I want to take the sort of photographs that make you question what's going on in the world. I take my camera with me everywhere now because whenever I didn't take it, I would invariably see something I needed to shoot. I have heroes that no one (apart from other photographers) have heard of. I want to be a Magnum photographer.

And then, of course, there's all the stuff I know about Salah. Not that he tells me as much as I tell him, but beneath the cool surface, he has a lot of dreams he doesn't want anyone to know about.

"Hey, Carol," Yo called out, "what country are we studying this term again?"

"Sometimes, I don't know why I bother," she replied, pointing to her board, with its now elaborately decorated map of Egypt.

Just before the bell rang, she said, "Would you come to the front of the class, Sam? I want to play a sadistic ritual game with you and humiliate you in front of your classmates." Or something to that effect.

"Yeah, sure," I agreed, only I could feel my text alert vibrate, so I had to check my BlackBerry first. I signaled for Carol to wait while I checked the message. It was from Holly agreeing to meet up.

Sounds cool! See you then, xxxHolly

I like to give the impression that there is nothing more to my life than the pursuit and conquest of girls. I know there's a lot more to life than girls, but it amuses me to think that everybody else figures I haven't worked that out yet. It gives me a cover. Salah always tells me that there's nothing to gain by letting everyone know everything about you.

I tossed the BlackBerry in my bag and eased myself out of my chair, to join Carol by the board.

She shoved a pile of papers at me. "You really don't deserve this trip, but pass these out."

I glanced through the pages before heading down the aisle to pass them out. They were forms and permission slips for a school trip to Egypt.

I waved them in the air for the class to see. "Hey, Salah, we're taking a road trip to your homeland!"

"*Al-hamdu Lillah!*" Salah whooped. Apparently, that's Egyptian for "totally awesome!"

CHAPTER 2

♥♥♥ OCTAVIA ♥♥♥

Queens Ladies College, London

*You can never go too far. It's when you don't go far enough
that you come unstuck.*

Coco Chanel once said, "You never know, maybe
that's the day you have a date with destiny. And it's
best to be as pretty as possible for destiny."

I always think of that when I'm getting ready to go
out. But school—what's up with that? How can you
dress prettily when you're forced to wear a crappy uni-
form that was designed by girl haters in another cen-
tury? You simply have to put destiny from your mind
when it comes to school.

Especially in geography. It's the most rubbish subject—
almost as pointless as the people who teach it. What on
earth are we meant to learn from a tragedy like Mr.
Menzies? Rosie believes geogers exists so that we can
get our daily texting over and done with, which I suppose

makes sense, but still they could have someone less odious overlooking our texting class. Apart from coming from the deepest, darkest Outer Zones of madness, Mr. Menzies is always staring with a beady eye over our texting.

That particular day I had a great deal on my mind. All my friends were devoting themselves to causes or goals—and I don't mean pulling boys and clothes. No, suddenly a passion for real goals like careers and real causes like suffering children had swept our school.

My family's secret impoverishment pretty much prohibited me from thinking about dreams and causes because it took so much energy just disguising myself as one of them—you know, People Who Don't Have to Worry About Money. My family is titled but that's only because one of my ancient ancestors did something wonderful for some king a few hundred years ago. It must have been a very wonderful thing because it's also the reason why we own the largest and oldest private house in Mayfair. Unfortunately there's absolutely no money left. This year, Papa paid my school fees rather than get the roof fixed. Christmas was spent coming up with inventive ways of moving buckets about the house. Of course, my father would never consider doing anything sensible like sell the crumbling ruin. The house is his cause and selling it would be desecrating over four hundred years of Geudenault history, which if you ask me is no great loss. The point is there is no money and I don't want to be pitied.

The Geudenaults' history is littered with loons and crackpots. Papa is quite potty himself, and Mumsy is too busy shifting buckets to catch the roof leaks and, of course, running tours of the house to feed us to get Papa to see sense. Also if I told my friends the truth about my non-existent trust fund, I couldn't keep up the fantasy, and actually it's my fantasy life that keeps my sunny disposition going. Reality is overrated.

Mr. Menzies was banging on about some geoger-ish nonsense, so I started downloading the latest episode of my favorite American drama because you have to wait weeks to get it in the UK and I hate wasting time. Impatience is a virtue, which is why I worship wireless broadband and we don't have it at home.

Rosie turned around and asked. "Did he just say we were going on a school trip to Egypt?"

I glared at her because Rosie is my best friend and she knows how I feel about school trips. She thinks it's because I'm eccentric, because she has no idea how stupidly poor we are.

She rolled her eyes. "We're not still doing the Inner Londres thing, are we, Octavia?" By *we*, she meant *me*. I invented a whole Outer London Zone Phobia so that people would imagine my refusal to visit their places in the country or go abroad was a delightful madness rather than the pointlessness of asking my broker-than-broke Papa for travel money.

Friends tried to blackmail me into going on last term's ski trip to Verbier but I stood firm. I'm made of tougher stuff than the average teen. My friends all tell me I go too far, but my broad life experience has proved that you can never go too far. It's in not going far enough that people come unstuck.

"Elegance is refusal!" I reminded Rosie.

"You do know you're mad, Octavia, right?"

"It's my signature stance and a girl does not sacrifice her signature, Rosie."

We were rudely interrupted by our lunatic teacher. "I will not tolerate chitchat in my class, Miss O'Brien! Turn around or get out!"

Rosie turned back to her laptop. I didn't have to see what she was doing to know she was composing. That's what she wants to do when she's a grown-up-type person. Compose. *Vogue* has already done a feature on her as the big thing to watch in classical music.

Rosie's weirdly techie and spends a lot of time in her head deconstructing Bach fugues, but she's still totally cool and stylish in an iconoclastic fashion refusenik sort of way. Who else could get away with a Mathew Williamson sequined tunic, *Myla* knickers, boots, a splash of clear nail varnish, a squirt of Fracas, and nothing else, without looking like a tart? No one but Rosie, that's who, because she's got that whole cream-skin-and-legs-that-go-on-forever thing going on.

That's why it's so off the wall that she's insecure about her looks. Everyone's always telling me I'm attractive. If only looks were everything. Mumsy is always saying that all girls my age are beautiful: "Darling, of course you're stunning, but at your age that's nothing special." I wonder if Mumsy thinks *anything* is special—apart from Papa, of course. She worships him.

Anyway, for some unfathomable reason, Rosie is convinced she's a pale shadow of moi, which is so not true. She looks like an aristo that hit Portobello Market a bit hard. In fact she's so stunning, it's hard to accept what a genius she is sometimes.

All my friends are super directed and bright. It's a bit disheartening really—their direction thing, I mean. Perdie wants to play polo for England, and Artimis is, like, the most artistic person in the world. She might have the figure and the looks of an artist's muse, but she's the demon with the brush.

All I have is a title, and let's face it, who cares about *that* when you can't even afford to meet up with friends for pizza? The days of trading on a title are long gone in Londres. And no, I don't want to be an It Girl. The very thought makes my brain bleed. I've done a few magazine shoots because I get to keep the shoes and clothes. Without freebies my fantasy would be totally over. I also have an old sewing machine and for years I've been making most of my own clothes (not that I let on to anyone). Of course, everyone would be madly impressed, but at Queens you need labels. God, I wish I was deep and unfathomable like Rosie—and rich. Seriously though, she has hidden depths where I have shallow puddles. If I didn't love her so much, I might even be jealous.

Halfway through my download, Mr. Menzies asked me what I knew about Egypt.

"With all due respect, sir, that question seems a bit cheeky. You've interrupted me mid-download," I teased.

Mr. Menzies loves sparring with me. It gives him a chance to show off his authority. Rosie's always telling me that he hates it, but I can tell he secretly likes it, because he always gives me really good grades, and according to my parents, he heaps praise on me at parent-teacher evenings.

Everybody muffled giggles. My posse—Rosie, Perdie, and Artimis—all looked round and shook their heads in warning.

"With all due respect, Octavia," Mr. Menzies replied sarcastically, "as earth-shatteringly important as your download may be, when you're in *my* class, you'll pay attention to *my* lecture. We're discussing Egypt and I've asked for your input."

"Mr. Menzies, you're such a learned gentleman. I'm sure I'd only embarrass myself if I started interrupting your lecture with my vapid input. Anyway, the last time I looked, Egypt was in the Outer Zones, and I am nothing if not a girl of principle, Mr. Menzies."

"You're on the fast track to being *sent* to the principal, that's what you are, missy," my mad little man riposted. He was looking at me in an explosive sort of way and the classroom had gone quiet. I shrugged. And then he roared. "Right, that's it! Go and see Mrs. Selecker. You're an intelligent enough girl, but I will not tolerate your insubordination in my class, Octavia!"

Whoops. I knew then I should have closed my mouth, but part of my whole image is maintaining insouciance while baiting teachers. I started this game when I was five because it made the class laugh and everyone thought I was too cool for school, daring to cheek teachers. Now I just can't stop. I've created this image I can't escape from. Still, a disciplinary letter home from Mrs. Selecker to Papa and Mama at this stage could be catastrophic for both them and me. I forget sometimes how much I *need* to be at this school.

I tried smiling sweetly, hoping to reverse his mood.

"Out!" he yelled so loudly the room shook.

I continued to smile at him, as calm as the sphinx. If you ignore cross people long enough, they usually wear themselves out. My madre has worn me out over the years with her patience.

"It's okay, Mr. Menzies. Let's just put your outburst

down to geogers stress, shall we, darling? I shan't report you and I'm sure everyone here is prepared to stay mum." I looked around at my posse and they nodded to show they were prepared to sweep Mr. Menzies's tantrum under the carpet of life. If the English can do one thing apart from stiff upper lips and stodgy puddings, it's pretending things didn't happen. Going on about things is so fret making.

That was when my dear old comrade in argument had a fit. And I mean a proper fit with flailing limbs, eye popping, and speaking in tongues—well, rude language anyway.

"Whoops a daisy!" I cried as Rosie, Perdie, and Artimis all dived out of their seats and restrained him before he managed to throttle me. Seriously, he was definitely about to attack me with his hairy man fists. There goes the stiff upper lip! And my hope that his anger would blow over.

I pretended I wasn't dying of nerves and made my way to the throne room of our head, with the decorum of a tsarina.

"Darling," I told Mrs. Selecker, settling myself in the Le Corbusier chaise longue that dominated her office.

Mrs. Selecker looked annoyed when I told her of Mr. Menzies's inexcusable lack of restraint. "I don't want to make a formal complaint," I added. "I just thought you'd best be aware of the situation in case any of the other pupils' parents wish to lay the case before the school's governing body."

Mrs. Selecker stood up and sighed heavily as she propped herself on the corner of her desk, revealing a well-toned thigh. "Is this about the Inner Zone thing again, Octavia? Because Mr. Menzies isn't the only one losing patience here," she told me.

She was wearing one of her five Chanel suits; each of them was a different color. She rotated them daily, which was perfectly respectable, but she'd let herself down once again with her shoes and tights. I was about to help her out with a little charitable advice, when she held up her hand in a stop signal. "No one wants to hear it anymore, Octavia. I have spoken to your mother and assured her that the school will cover the cost of your trip. Like it or not, you are to go on this Egyptian trip."

At her mention of school charity, I pulled a nail file from my pocket and began filing my nails so she couldn't see the tears banking up behind my eyes. "That's ever so kind of you, darling," I told her, "but it's not an issue of money. This is a matter of principle. Not leaving the Inner Zones is my cause, darling, and without our causes, what are we?"

She spoke to me in her stern voice. "Octavia. Listen to me, and stop 'darling' me."

"Darling?" I cried, aggrieved.

"Octavia, I'm serious. This whole Inner Zone obsession was cute for a while. We all laughed when you proselytized your Zone One stance on the Channel Four documentary. I admit I found your argument compelling in a vacuous sort of way. But Octavia, it is not reality."

"And what's so fabulous about reality?" I asked her pointedly.

CHAPTER 3

❤❤❤ SALAH ❤❤❤

Luxor, Egypt

*My guys think the only point to school trips is hot foreign girls
and getting wasted. But Egypt wasn't foreign to me.
I still thought of it as home.*

I think it only hit me how awesome this trip would be
when we were circling Luxor and I saw the patch-
work of fields that hem the Nile and the ancient city
hewn from the desert below.

I hadn't been to Egypt since I was a kid, when my
grandparents were still alive, but I suddenly felt I could
taste the sweet bazbooka my grandma used to make.
We'd stayed in the Old Winter Palace on our last visit,
but I'd spent my time in the gardens, lying under the
palm fronds and looking up at the dusky pink sky and
thinking of nothing.

I still do a lot of that. Think of nothing. Emptying
my mind helps me cope with the craziness of life.

"Hey dude, why so quiet? What are you thinking

about?" Sam asked as he put his camera away and put up his tray table for landing.

"Wondering what these girls from London will be like," I lied, because that's what Sam would like to hear. I knew it was pathetic, but I seriously wanted my boys to *get* Egypt, Sam especially. Not just because he was my best friend, but if anyone in our group was going to see beyond the obvious, it was Sam. He might goof around and act like all that mattered to him was girls and good times, but that's all it was. An act.

I wasn't going to obsess about it. The souls of my friends were too rooted in Manhattan. Every school trip was the same. Last year we'd done Florence, the year before that the UK, and next year we'd go somewhere else. The point of foreign trips to my boys was hot foreign girls and getting wasted. Afterward we always went back to our lives in New York as if nothing had happened, because life outside Manhattan, it just wasn't real.

As the plane bumped and bounced down on the desert tarmac, we were thrown forward and all the gear from the overhead compartments started flying around the cabin. The guys and I were laughing as we dodged bags. Carol's screams pierced the cabin, and as we finally slowed to a halt, the Egyptian passengers all clapped and cheered.

Sam grinned. "What are they cheering for? That was the most pathetic landing in the history of aviation!"

"They're glad to be here, maybe," I told him.

"Your people are crazy, Salah," he told me, rubbing the back of my head.

"Thanks, Sam."

"And you know how much I *love* crazy."

. . .

We taxied across the tarmac to the terminal, where a sea of crumpled, grumpy tourists and realistically resigned Egyptians searched for purpose and direction in the chaos. It was hot and dusty and the police in their black woolen uniforms, clutching AK-47s, seemed to be disorganizing rather than organizing the lines.

But within a few minutes, our tour rep swooped down on me and introduced himself as Mustafa. I figured he thought I was the teacher as I was the only one wearing a suit—my father's influence. My father respects the craftsmanship of the hand-stitched suit. He likes to have the best of everything but never the flashiest. I like that about him. I mean, I'm seriously not into fashion, but I do appreciate the effort of craftsmanship. In a world of technology and labels, where everything is mass-produced for mass consumption, there's something timeless and comforting about someone going to the trouble to construct and stitch an entire suit by hand.

I pointed out Carol and Ms. Doyle to Mustafa and explained that they were the ones in charge, but Carol's hippie getup and Ms. Doyle's army fatigues obviously discouraged him, so he continued to deal with me. We'd fallen into Arabic and he was speaking to me as if I were his senior.

Eventually Ms. Doyle came over. She walked like a lumberjack, her fatigues set off by an enormous fanny pack crammed with high-energy survival foods and other supplies. "I'm Ms. Doyle, the history teacher. Are you Mr. Mohammed from Egypt Educational Tours?" she growled.

Mustafa seemed afraid. I explained to Ms. Doyle that Mohammed would be meeting us at the boat and that Mustafa was just our reception guy. After I'd formally introduced everyone, Mustafa ushered us through the arrivals terminal and customs like we were VIPs.

"I'm liking this country," Sam announced as we were fast-tracked past the heaving mass of resentful tourists. "This is the first time I've gone through customs in another country and not been made to feel like an American criminal."

"Yeah, these guys are fools, man. We could be anyone," Yo joked. At seven feet tall, he towered over everybody.

"Hey, I *am* someone," Astin reminded him, running his hand over his crew cut and giving Yo a shove into a bunch of jocks. Yo was shoved back by the jocks, and before long there was a whole lot of shoving and Ms. Doyle told us to cut it out.

As far as we were concerned, this was a school trip and Ms. Doyle was going to have to get used to being ignored. Our shoving attracted the interest of two policemen holding hands nearby. It's a perfectly common thing in Egypt for men to hold hands and kiss one another on the cheek in greeting—for us it's more acceptable than slapping another guy on the back. The two policemen wandered over and halfheartedly menaced us with their AK-47s. Their hearts might not have been in it, but coming from New York, we weren't used to being challenged with automatic weapons—be it halfheartedly or otherwise. Suddenly everyone stood at attention, though I could tell by the look on Ms. Doyle's face that she was wondering how to get her hands on an automatic weapon. I explained to the police that we were only fooling around and that Ms. Doyle was just an American tool and they laughed and wandered off hand in hand.

Mustafa didn't find my remarks about Ms. Doyle funny though. He asked me where I was from. A few questions later and he'd worked out who my family was. I could tell from the look on his face that he was processing that I was the son of one of Egypt's most famous men. I suddenly saw myself as the spoiled rich kid that he clearly thought I was.

"Have we just witnessed gay policing at its best?" Astin asked, nudging me.

I knew he was confused but I couldn't resist messing with his head. "Wanna hold my hand, Astin baby?" I offered, making a grab for his hand. "We're finally free to love one another in a totally man-on-man way." Astin pulled his hand away from mine.

"No, don't worry, dude. Holding hands is just customary here," I reassured him.

Astin looked astonished. "You've never tried to hold my hand before!"

"Well, when in Egypt, do as the Egyptians do."

"Maybe not," he replied, slapping me on the back.

. . .

By the time we'd all piled into the bus, the combination of desert heat and the rhythmic beat of the Egyptian music pumping out of the bus's stereo sent a party vibe rippling through our group. We all started grooving to the music as we tried to get signals on our BlackBerrys and cells. Yo had reattached his VR visor and was swaying around in his own virtual Egyptian world. He was actually playing a game called Temple Terror: The Pharaoh's Peril, and he was already on level five. Yo's view on reality was that it was "all relative."

Ms. Doyle started speaking to the driver about something, but the guy screeched out of the parking lot, sending her flying onto Carol's lap. In that moment, seeing the butch Ms. Doyle flailing around on Carol's lap, I decided I never wanted to leave Egypt.

Our driver had a take-no-prisoners approach to driving. This included weaving his way into the oncoming traffic and taking the other cars by surprise. It was a battle of wills and a war of horns and hair raising for everyone on the bus.

"This is total anarchy!" Astin said as our driver leaned on his horn. "Are we even driving on the right side, dude?"

"It's all relative," I told him.

"Hey, check out the donkey," Sam called out as we passed a depressed donkey pulling a wooden cart laden with a tired pile of vegetables and two disgruntled guys in galabias arguing. Sam pulled out his camera and started snapping.

Astin replied, "Yeah, you don't see enough donkeys in New York if you ask me, which, by the way, none of you ever do."

I wrapped Astin in a headlock and gave him a fake pounding.

Luckily our drive of death ended as we squealed to a halt along the Nile. Small river-cruise boats were docked next to one another. Mustafa pointed out the *Nefertiti* as ours, but he shouldn't have bothered. We were already glued to the sight of long-limbed girls in bikinis stretched out on lounge chairs on the upper deck.

As we walked the red carpet leading to the gangplank, Sam waved up to them, whistled, and yelled, "Whoa, baby!" in a bad impression of a British accent.

The jocks yelled out similar cries of desperate longing, but even though we were well within hearing distance and the girls must have seen and heard us clambering to get aboard, none of them so much as waved.

"I'm guessing snooty Brits," Astin said. "If anyone's asking."

"Which none of us are," Sam pointed out, and we started joking around again, acting as if we weren't all obsessed with the girls. Which couldn't have been further from the truth. Even I was mildly curious.

CHAPTER 4

♥♥♥ ROSIE ♥♥♥

The perfect antidote for an introvert like me was a madder-than-mad friend who drove me up the wall half the time . . . and made me feel like a princess the rest.

Hell is other people—according to the great French thinker Jean-Paul Sartre, who is not a man I greatly admire. I can't say I'm a fan of the short, overly opinionated, Champagne-Stalinist type. But still, from the moment we embarked on that school trip, I could see what he meant.

Hell was Octavia. She's my best friend and I worship her mad little ways—most of the time. Where I am introverted and a bit of a musical swot, Octavia is, well . . . Octavia is a force of nature. Mostly in an iconoclastic, hilarious way. Like the way she "darlings" teachers. Anyone else would get completely told off for that, but Octavia manages to slip through the punishment noose time and time again. Things always go well for Octavia, and I admire her daring, but sometimes she drives me up the wall. Especially when it comes to boys. Namely the way all the boys I fancy are crazy for her and I end up with their sidekick, which makes me feel like Octavia's sidekick. She has absolutely no idea I feel this way.

I think when she first came to Queens we were all swept away by her sense of entitlement. I mean, we are all relatively privileged, going to a top London private school, but as the daughter of one of Britain's oldest families, Octavia was born knowing she would never be asked to do a tap of work and so she never has. Not that she ever goes on about her family or her money or anything. Actually, she's incredibly mum about the whole thing. A lot of girls would flash their title as much as their cleavage. But then Octavia doesn't need to wield her title, she only has to bat her lashes and the world falls at her feet.

It is kind of cool having a friend who's unabashed about speaking her mind. Octavia can rinse anyone in any argument, and for someone as—well, let's face it—wimpish as me, that's an impressive quality. I kind of live in my own head a lot. I like to break up a melodic line of Bach into four bits and muck about with the bits in my head. I invert some, switch others around and break them with a bar, and then interweave them with the original.

Sad, I know.

It's hard to explain to other people and so I rarely do. Which I think is for the best. That's why Octavia's good for me. The perfect antidote for an introverted swot like me is a madder-than-mad friend who makes me dare rather than cower. She drags me out of my head and reminds me there is another world outside musical notes. I think I would be a total freak without her. The best thing about her is the way she makes me laugh. Well, most of the time. On other occasions her eccentricities have been known to drive me into realms of despair.

Since we'd heard about this trip, she'd been in a slump. I suspect it wasn't really the usual Outer Zone Hell thing as she claimed. I wondered if it wasn't something to do with her parents. When I stayed with her once I got the impression money was a bit of an issue, but Octavia's never said anything, so I haven't. Anyway I'm probably reading too much into things. An old mattress and worn curtains aren't really such a big deal. Nor is lack of central heating. I guess I just presumed that Octavia's family would have a chauffeur-driven Roller but her parents don't even own a car.

My mother found this incredibly strange. "Who doesn't own a car?" she exclaimed when I told them about my stay. They're actually dreadful snobs, my parents. But then my father said, "Those old families are often obsessively careful about avoiding anything flashy. Besides, damn sensible not having a car in London. Not to mention good for the environment." This from a man who collects vintage cars and drives a Range Rover the hundred yards to his office every day! Hypocrite. As if he imagined that I didn't know he was only saying all this rubbish because of Octavia's title.

Finally, the coach bearing our cargo of boys pulled up. I'd been counting on the American boys to cheer up Octavia, but by the time they finally started clambering out of their coach, even that sliver of hope began to vanish. She looked disdainful as the boys whistled and called up to us. None of us moved from our loungers. We didn't want to appear too keen. But we all looked knowingly at one another and grinned, imagining the pull fest that lay ahead, once we'd checked out who was fit and who was fit to forget.

But not Octavia.

I climbed off my lounger and sneaked a peep over the deck to check out the last of the boys as they walked up the gangplank.

"I think one of the Americans is wearing a suit," I mentioned. Octavia loves good tailoring. God knows why. At our age only guys in pretentious bands wear suits.

"I bet it's machine made," she replied, not even bothering to peer over her sunglasses.

As long as a boy is Savile Rowed to the eyeballs and fit, she'll pull him. There isn't a boy on the planet that doesn't want Octavia the moment he lays eyes on her. Many a London boy has shed his Ralphies for a bespoke suit simply to catch Octavia's eye.

Sometimes I wish I had a less attractive friend, which I know sounds really mean. But seriously, it's no fun being second prize.

With her thick mane of glossy black hair, green cat's eyes, and breathtaking figure, she makes every other girl she stands beside look bad. Add to that the fact she always dresses in the most spellbindingly fabulous way, and you have to wonder why any girl in her right mind would want to be seen next to her. She does make me laugh though—and force me to do things I'd otherwise never dare. Octavia doesn't believe in the concept of "too far." Her favorite line from her favorite film, *Ferris Bueller's Day Off*, is, "You can never go too far."

Me? I'm sometimes afraid of my own shadow.

I put my iPod in and listened with a critical ear to a piece I'd composed for my music tutor. The piece was due to be handed in soon, and I'd already used my extension, but it was still missing something. The more I heard it, the more discordant it sounded.

Mr. Menzies climbed onto the upper deck, looking like a puddle of tea in his polyester khaki safari suit. "Right, girlies! Enough sunning yourselves!"

Octavia turned onto her tummy.

"Come on, chop, chop. We're not here for a holiday. Cover yourselves up now, this is a school trip, not a harem. The boys have arrived, so we'll convene in half an hour in the lounge bar for a welcome drink and a discussion of our program." He really is such a fool. Who says words like *convene* anyway? Also he used his fingers to parenthesize the word *bar* as the bar would not be serving alcohol to us. Obviously the teachers would drink themselves stupid the entire week. They always do on school trips.

"What do you think the boys will be like?" I asked as I set off down the stairs from the upper deck.

"American?" Octavia replied. "Totally, like, totally, like, *American*, man," she added in a perfect American accent.

"Yar, what's up with the way they talk? Do you think they'll really call one another 'dude' and high-five one another?" Perdita asked.

"Frankly I don't give a damn as long as there are some fitties amongst them," Octavia declared. "It's not as if I want them for their conversation, darling," she added as we strolled into the air-conditioned bar and came face-to-face with a godlike boy in a bespoke suit and rubbish trainers, stretched out in one of the booths.

He looked up from his newspaper and smiled and for

some reason I thought his smile was just for me. Which, of course, it couldn't have been.

He was opening and closing his mouth but I was so mesmerized that it took forever to decipher what it was he was saying. By the time I worked it out, I was drooling with desire. He had introduced himself and was asking what I was listening to.

"Erm, well, that is, well, nothing. No one you'd know," I blabbered away uselessly.

"She's listening to herself," Octavia told him, flicking her hair seductively. "Rosie's always listening to herself. That's the nature of genius, the pursuit of perfection. She's the most brilliant composer! Scarily talented in fact."

Octavia was being genuinely nice. She's always singing my praises and trying to help me get over my shyness with boys, but I was feeling too freakishly awkward to cope with this godlike boy without him knowing I had a scary talent.

He smiled. "So, can I listen to you?" he asked, stretching out his long fingers for my iPod.

"It's not finished yet," I explained. "It needs something. It needs . . . a lot in fact . . ." I babbled on, but he'd already placed the earpiece in his ear. And he closed his eyes and smiled, and as I waited for his verdict, I fell madly, inexorably, impossibly in love with him.

"I love that key change at the end," he said to me, passing my iPod back.

And that was that. There *was* no key change at the end, but a key change at the end *was* precisely what it needed. He was the answer to all my dreams. Unaware that cupid's arrow had pierced my heart, Octavia strolled across to my dream boy as if gliding down a runway. "Nice suit. Gieves and Hawke?" she enquired.

"Ozwald Boateng," he replied disinterestedly, his eyes still fixed on me.

"Very nice," she purred, swinging her legs into the booth and snuggling her bikini-clad figure up beside him.

He looked over at me. I was still rooted to the spot. It was clear that Octavia had staked her claim, and normally that would be enough for me to back off and climb back into my box. But not then. At that moment I wanted to scratch out her eyes, and I am so not normally like that.

"Octavia," she announced as if her name were a promise—or a threat. Then she kissed him on each cheek. "Loving the suit, loving the sun, loving you, darling," she declared.

"Salah," the guy replied, and maybe I was delusional, but I thought he moved slightly away from her.

The rest of us were all about to leave Octavia to

work her spell, but Salah called out, "Hey, music girl, aren't you going to join us?"

Octavia said, "Rosie is madly shy, darling."

The worst of it was, she was right. I was too shy to join them. There was nothing I could do but leave Octavia to it. I decided to go back to my computer and effect the key change in the last passage.

· · ·

When we came up from changing, the rest of the guys were already in the bar. Octavia was still in her bikini and Mr. Menzies was giving her a piece of his mind. She ignored him as she sipped a mint tea and fluttered her madly long eyelashes at Salah, who had been joined in a booth by three other fitties drooling shamelessly over her.

Both sides of the bar had floor-to-ceiling windows with views of the Nile on one side and Luxor town on the other. It was madly modern, more like the sort of uber-trendy bar you find in London, where you have to be a member to get in. The staff were all in black tie and were wandering around with glasses of iced mint tea, a red drink called *karkaday*, and freshly squeezed orange juice.

I sat down with Octavia though she barely acknowledged me. It wasn't because she was being mean. She'd sighted her prey and that was that. She probably wouldn't notice me again until she'd pulled Salah. And

I can't blame her. I could easily have got lost in a boy like that.

. . .

We'd all taken our seats, Octavia and the boys in booths on the Nile side of the bar and girls on the shore side. Off in the corner stood a large woman in a bizarre hippie getup and an Egyptian man whose Indiana Jones–inspired attire was complete with flak jacket and hat. Our diminutive history teacher, Mr. Bell, who was over a hundred years old if he was a day, was wandering about the room passing out itinerary sheets. He looked the height of madosity in a pair of high-tech binoculars and a straw hat that had a special compartment in the crown in which to carry water.

Monday, Day 1
Welcome aboard the *Nefertiti*

Sunset: 17:56
12:30 Welcome drinks and discussion of itinerary
13:00 Lunch in the Nefertiti restaurant
14:00 Coach to Temple of Karnak and Temple of
     Luxor
17:00 Tea served on the pool deck
20:00 Dinner in Nefertiti restaurant

22:30 Whirling Dervish and Belly Dance Show in
        Upstairs Ankh bar
Overnight in Luxor

Everyone immediately began reading their itinerary, but as hard as I tried, I couldn't take my eyes from Salah. Not even humming a little lovely, lovely Bach could stop me from noticing his lashes sweep across his honey brown cheekbones or that he had shiny black hair just like Octavia's. But it was more than that. He had suggested a key change. He had taken an interest in something other than the way I looked—or rather, the way Octavia looked. It was awful. And the truth was, they looked brilliant together. I could groan with the unfairness of it all. Why was I standing in line behind Octavia—well, everyone really—when the looks and charisma were handed out?

Salah's long, tapered fingers rested peacefully on the table. His hands mesmerized me. I have known a lot of boys, and one thing about them is they never stay still. Never. Repose is not something you associate with sixteen-year-old boys, and yet that's what Salah had. Repose by the bucketload.

I found myself stealing glances at him until he eventually noticed, at which point I went bright red—which, given my Irish complexion and strawberry-blond hair, was never a good look. After that, I studiously avoided eye contact with him and fiddled with my BlackBerry even though I had no signal.

The big woman in the hippie getup introduced herself as Carol and began to drone on in a ghastly nasal twang.

"First of all, let me introduce myself to the girls of Queens." And then, I swear this is true, she gave us a little bow as if we were actual queens or something. "My name's Carol, and this gentleman beside me is our Egyptologist, Mo-ham-med." She exaggerated the name clearly as if she were speaking to infants. "He'll be leading the tours and answering any questions you might have, and I'm sure there'll be a heck of a lot of those."

That set us girls off in a piss take of American accents. Honestly, I know we're immersed in American culture through film and television, but it doesn't make American accents sound less funny, does it? In fact, maybe that's why they make me giggle so—because it's like meeting a television character in real life.

Mohammed stepped forward then, took off his Indiana Jones hat, and grinned broadly. I was so loving him. He just looked so happy and enthused. Normally I would have shared this thought with Octavia, but she was still all over Salah.

"I'm the guy who'll be giving you all the bloody blah, blah, blah about Egyptian history," Mohammed explained. "You know what blah, blah, blah means? You bloody well will by the time we finish. Then you will say, 'Mohammed, shut the bloody hell up with the bloody blah, blah, blah.'"

All the students laughed and clapped, but Carol waved for us to settle down.

"Yes, Mohammed, thank you." She coughed awkwardly. "As you can see from your programs," she continued, slightly flustered, "after lunch we'll be taking a bus to Karnak Temple. Now it will be very hot, so please apply plenty of sunscreen and wear a hat. Ms. Doyle, Mr. Bell, and Mr. Menzies, my two British counterparts on this tour, will be accompanying us."

Ms. Doyle, who was dressed like a freak from a war film and was munching on a high-energy bar, lumbered over to join Carol. I bet she ate girls for breakfast. Carol embraced her as if Ms. Doyle were a tree. "I am sure Mohammed will have a lot to share with us, but Ms. Doyle is also an Egyptology buff herself, and will have a heck of a lot to tell you. She won't mind sharing her time if you have any questions, as long as you respect her personal space on the boat. We teachers need our leisure time too, you know."

Again, all of the girls from Queens burst into laughter at hearing the American use of the word *leisure*. The guys looked at us like we were maddies, so we all quieted down. As miraculously good-looking as they were, I was beginning to worry they might be a super nerdy lot and took their teachers seriously, which might turn out to be a bit of a yawn.

Carol continued. "Mr. Menzies, a fellow geography teacher from Eng-ga-land, could you present yourself, please?"

I looked at Mr. Menzies in his safari suit. His khaki trousers were actually shorty shorts exposing the knobbly white knee of the Englishman. Not our best ambassador. He giggled girlishly, which made the boys from New York crack up, and I began to relax and think they just might be cool after all.

Mr. Menzies stood up and joined Carol and Ms. Doyle at the front of the room. He was so embarrassing, chuckling away lecherously at the two of them as if he'd never seen such hot totty. It really was too sick-making for words and almost made me forget all about Octavia and Salah.

Mr. Menzies gave Carol a nudge with his elbow as he said, "Thank you, Carol. Sterling job, sterling job and I think, for the purpose of our trip here, and in the spirit of cross-cultural relations, you can all call me Nigel."

"Oh darling, do we have to?" Octavia whined, stretched out catlike in the booth. Seriously, she was all over Salah, and with her dark mane of shiny hair and tanned lithe body, she bore a striking resemblance to Cleopatra. I could hardly blame Salah for being smitten. Still, it made my head spin with crossness.

"Yes, Octavia, on this you will fall in line with everyone else," Nigel told her, puffing out his chest manfully—for the sake of Carol I suspected. "And while we're at it, you can go and get dressed. You are a Queens lady. Show a bit of decorum."

Oh poor, poor innocent Nigel. He really had no idea.

CHAPTER 5

♥♥ SAM ♥♥

Karnak

*At some stage in life, you have to sign a
peace treaty with your desires.*

The girls were all hot. Two of them were sizzling. So
was the heat. We were wandering around the Karnak Temple complex, standing in the insane tempera-
ture, listening to Mohammed as he tried to explain the
complex history of the place. He was dressed like an in-
trepid explorer and looked like the real deal compared
to the other guides in their Lacoste tees and trendy sunglasses. Everyone looked so modern that it was pretty
hard to believe we were actually standing among some
of the oldest ruins in the world. Mohammed was pas-
sionate about his subject, but I was checking out the history of Karnak on my BlackBerry because it was hard to
hear him over the noise of all the other guides. Yo was
stumbling around the temple in his VR visor, bumping

into walls, experiencing his own virtual Egypt. He said it "enhanced the real experience." Given that he wasn't experiencing the real thing in his visor, I wondered how it could be enhanced, but whatever.

Mohammed moved us along as he tried to explain why the Karnak Temples had been built. The teachers kept interrupting him, showing off to each other. The girls kept disappearing behind pillars, chatting and fiddling with their own BlackBerrys. The entire temple complex was alive with the sound of tourists, their guides, and the ring of cell phones. I started to take some shots with my Leica, but it was so crowded it was difficult to use and I reverted to my digital.

Eventually I lined up this brilliant shot of a couple of the guys leaning against one of the hieroglyphed columns, scrolling down their BlackBerrys. I didn't even have to ask them to do anything. It was a perfectly constructed natural shot, exposing the historic temple complex in a totally now way. They were all discussing their scores on Yo's infamous Hottie Chart. He'd e-mailed the chart to the class on the bus to the temple.

Yo had been doing his Hottie Charts since the ninth grade. Here's how it worked: All the London girls' names were listed, and we then gave each of them a score so that everyone knew where everyone else's intentions lay. Then we cc-ed everyone else our scores. We had only a week, after all, so we couldn't exactly afford to leave anything to chance. I'd already filled in my scores and cc-ed the class. I'd given Octavia a top score of Off the Scale. So had everyone, except for Salah, who has never filled in one of Yo's Hottie Charts. In his words, "they're lame." No one really expects Salah to do anything other than stand apart, but Yo always tries to convince him to participate. Salah usually rolls his eyes.

Mohammed was getting increasingly exasperated with the interruptions and kept pulling on the toggle of his hat. "The temple complex, how long you think it take to build?"

"Well, Rome wasn't built in a day," Nigel quipped to chuckles from some of the other teachers.

"No, not a day! They take bloody two thousand years to build!" Mohammad cried.

"The builders must have been exhausted by the end of that," Carol added, and Nigel clapped his approval.

Poor Mohammed. He was already competing with dozens of other guides, who were giving the same spiel in Russian, French, Italian, Japanese, Spanish, and God knows what else, without having to battle our own teachers and their lame jokes. I went back to taking surreptitious digital shots of people in the temple complex. I loved the contrast of modern technology and the ruins. I took a few stealthy shots of Octavia, who was comparing the hieroglyphic pictures of the goddesses to models on the catwalk.

"I am so going to channel Hathor," she was saying to Rosie.

"Many people say this is where Rameses II, who was married to Nefertari, signed the world's first peace treaty. Yes, this was over three thousand years ago," Mohammed said proudly.

"That was with the Hittites, wasn't it?" Mr. Bell interrupted, taking the bottle of water from his hat and undoing the cap. "And as I recall it was Rameses who came off rather badly from that battle. The Hittites wiped the floor with Rameses the so-called Great." He laughed at his own joke.

Poor Mohammed. He tightened the toggle on his hat and ushered us into the Great Temple of Amun. He did not look happy. In fact, he looked like he was entering the Temple of Doom.

My cell rang. It was my mom. I assured her that I hadn't been shot at yet. It was the third call since I'd arrived in Egypt. As I was saying another long good-bye and promising to watch out for gunmen, Octavia sidled up to Salah and me and took our hands. "So, darlings, are you loving Mohammed?"

"Oh yeah, loving him, darling," I told her. What I was loving was the feel of her hand in mine.

"I think he's gorge, don't you, Salah?" she asked, spritzing herself with Evian.

"Yeah, I think he's going to be very interesting."

"I know exactly what you mean, darling. He has a sensitive, vulnerable nature. I think we should save him from the teachers, don't you? They're being so know-it-all-ish and horrid. Let's show him a good time."

"What do you have in mind?" I asked, hoping she might mean something fun, but she had danced off and joined Rosie again. They were both dressed in skimpy shorts. Octavia's were shocking pink linen with a black silk belt around the waist. Rosie's were a peach-colored satin with an orange Hermes scarf. They were both wearing heels that were totally impractical but they didn't seem worried about ruining them as we trawled around the hundreds of acres of awesomely large temples. They giggled when they slipped in the sand, they giggled when they squirted one another with Evian. I took some quick shots before they noticed me photographing them.

When we got to the obelisk of Hatshepsut, Mohammed asked, "So, what would you think of woman who wants to erect two golden obelisks to her father?"

"I'd say she was a really, really loving daughter," Octavia replied earnestly.

Mohammed looked confused. "No! She was bloody crazy woman. She claims she is daughter of god Amun! You can't be daughter of *god*! No. This, we cannot accept."

"I accepted that my father was a god when he gave

me my first black Amex," Perdie said. "Perhaps one day I'll build him an obelisk."

"They're very phallic, aren't they? I'm sure as a banker he'd love that," Octavia added, squirting Perdie with Evian.

Mohammed drew the cord on his hat even tighter. The poor guy was close to strangling himself.

Karnak was a cool place. Big, awesomely big, but so crowded with tourists from every nation it felt like a theme park—like maybe the statues of the gods or the pillars might double up as thrill rides. I took dozens of shots of the police, who were everywhere in their black woolen uniforms clutching their AK-47s. One dude kept loading and unloading his cartridge magazine, which was disturbing, especially after my mother's call. I got a shot of his cartridge belt when he dumped it on the ground at one point.

Salah as usual had all the girls falling at his feet. Not that he seemed aware of it. Octavia was getting the lion's share of attention. She managed to ooze sex appeal while being funny, which was a huge turn-on. There was this one point when we spotted a couple of dozen people all dressed in white, their hands placed on an enormous black stone scarab beetle. Octavia said to Carol, who was wearing a white sari, "Darling, look over there, your brethren!" Carol muttered something inaudible and then Octavia went over to the group and pointed Carol out to them. I don't know what she said, but they reached out their arms to Carol, and if Nigel hadn't interceded, I think we might have lost Carol to a cult.

"Sometimes, madam, you go too far," Nigel told Octavia.

"Don't be silly. I've told you, you can never go too far!"

Nigel patted his sweating brow with a white handkerchief and said, "Yes, yes, yes, Octavia, just have some respect for the, erm, what you call it? Culture."

"Oh, do try to be less of a bore," Octavia whispered to Nigel. "You'll never pull Carol if you don't loosen up a bit."

Astin nudged me, raising one eyebrow. "Can you believe that girl?"

I was about to answer but Octavia had heard him and shimmied up to him singing, "You're unbelievable!" It was as close to a lap dance as Astin had ever had, and it sent the jocks into a frenzy. They started yelling "You go, girl!" and taking pictures of her with their cell phones.

"Peasants," Octavia sneered teasingly. I jumped away from Astin and the jocks, hoping to single myself out as a nonpeasant and grinned like an idiot only to have Astin and the jocks shove me aside. Not one of my proudest moments.

Afterward, we sat in a Bedouin tented café, which got us out of the heat. We drank Coke and a hot, sweet, milk-shakelike drink called *salep*. Octavia smoked a *shisha*, a sort of water pipe with fragrant tobacco. She made it look ridiculously erotic. The teachers were all talking with Mohammed further off so they didn't see her, but even if they had, I wondered what they could have said to reprimand her. I was guessing none of them wanted to go there.

Before long, Octavia had attracted a crowd of local tour reps and hustlers. The girls I knew back in Manhattan would have freaked out if a crowd of Egyptian men had swarmed them, but Octavia chatted quite happily with them. The more outrageous she was, the more hilarious they seemed to find her.

I elbowed Salah and pointed to Octavia. "I think you're in there, man."

He was sipping on a glass of *salep* and sucking on his own *shisha*. "She's not my type."

"Come on, Octavia's not a *type,* she's a goddess."

Salah shrugged. "Whatever. She doesn't do it for me. But hey, if you like her, Sam, go work your mojo."

I was about to grovel in gratitude to him, when Rosie came and joined us. She perched on a carpeted stool beside Salah. She was wearing a quirky vintage black lace shirt over a lime green bikini top. She was definitely hot in a classic sort of way; leggy, long strawberry-blond curls. Not in the same league as Octavia, but cute just the same.

Salah grabbed a passing waiter and called to him in Arabic.

"Wow, that's so cool! You speak Arabic?" Rosie asked.

I listened to their conversation while I went through the pictures I'd been taking. "Yeah, it kinda helps that I was born here."

I thought it was sweet the way she blushed. "Wow, that must be amazing. What a cool place to be born."

Salah laughed. "Thanks, I think so."

"I really like the way Arabic sounds. I mean, it actually does sound like an old language doesn't it?"

I looked up and watched Salah's face as he considered this. "I suppose it does," he said, and smiled at her as if she'd made him think about his native tongue for the first time.

We all sat back and took in the scene. Rosie looked around the café. "This place is so civilized. Don't you love it? How can you bear living in America?"

While Salah and Rosie chatted about Egyptian customs, I drifted off into my own thoughts. Octavia still had the Egyptians in hysterics, and her audience was growing by the minute. Salah had given me the green light on her, which should have made me feel easy. What actually happened was that for the first time since middle school, I felt insecure. And for the life of me, I didn't know why.

I've been cruising on a wave of self-confidence since I was about fifteen and started dating one of Manhattan's hottest ice queens. Some people think I'm a smart ass and sometimes I agree. It's true that things are uncomplicated for me when it comes to girls. There are no serious ups and downs, just beginnings and ends. I'm not saying that's how I wanted it, it's just how it was. I had never imagined myself to be *in love*. Whatever that means.

I'd seen guys in crisis over girls but I'd never experienced it and never envied it. I felt sorry for the lovesick schmucks. I'm saying all this in retrospect, of course. I can't help wondering if I wasn't overrating the uncomplicatedness of my love life when I look at the guy I was before my life was turned upside down by the prospect of Octavia.

CHAPTER 6

♥♥♥ OCTAVIA ♥♥♥

NO is only an option, one we are all free to choose to refuse.

T he Salah situation isn't going well, Rosie. I fear you may need to give things a bit of a push," I told her after we'd showered off the temple dust. We were both sitting on our beds with one towel wrapped around our torsos and another wound turban-style around our hair.

I took a snap of Rosie with my mobile. For a while I had managed to make *not* having a mobile an admirable eccentricity, but eventually even I had to succumb to the lure of mod technology. Now I'm on pay-as-you-go—not that anyone in my world would even know what that concept is. I doubt Papa knows what a mobile is—he probably thinks it's a house on wheels. I made the money for my mobile by taking tour groups around the house for Mumsy last summer. Now I know why she's such a cloth-headed nutty darling. Taking those tours would turn the stoutest mind soft.

I checked the image on the screen but the result wasn't very promising. Rosie's eyes looked beady and cross. I showed her. "That's not a happy snap, darling, what's the matter with you?" I asked.

"Oh, it's just the heat," she assured me. Rosie hated the heat, it made her skin prickle. That's why she's the only friend I've ever had to Farringdon House, where everything is cold and damp, thanks to the fact that the central heating packed up five years ago. She absolutely adored it. She didn't even mind that the beds were like wet porridge while I know from personal experience the bliss of sleeping on the downy heaven of her mattress in Chelsea. She went down very well with the madre and padre too, but then they get out so little they'd probably be happy to have a balloon on a piece of string to tea.

"I'm loving it. The heat," I told her. "I'm going to get so tanned, but because you're my bestest friend in the world, Rosie, I will apply sunblock all over you and keep you under a parasol." That made her laugh. "But back to Salah. He's obviously too shy to pull me, so you'll have to do that subtle shove thing you do so well. Red or Pink?" I asked as I held up two bottles of nail polish.

"Pink. Sorry, Octavia, but I don't know about this."

"About the color, or the Salah thing?"

"The Salah thing."

I gave her my most insistent look. "Of course you know, darling. I've done it for you *loads* of times," I reminded her, which was true. Rosie was a complete ruin when it came to affairs of the heart.

"I know, but you're you and I'm, well, I'm not a bit like you, basically," she said.

"Now you're not making sense. Have you been reading French literature again?"

Rosie flopped on her bed. "Look, Octavia, you're my dearest friend, but, shoving boys into your arms is not my style."

I waved her objection away and started on my toes with the red. Red is so much more the color of pulling. "Look, we only have a week, and if shoving is what's required, we must roll up our sleeves and shove. It's not a style statement, it's a necessity," I pointed out. I can be a very practical girl when situations demand it. That's what comes from growing up in a crumbling ruin.

Rosie groaned and kicked her legs in the air to vent her frustration.

"Don't worry, Rosie," I reassured her. "I'll feed you your lines and you can deliver them in your own adorable way. He's probably just ultra shy and weird like you. I mean, who knows what goes on in the American psyche? I don't even think they have a word for pulling. They have that funny dating thing happening, and I don't see how we can waste time on a dating regime when we've only got a week." I held up my foot and wriggled my toes to admire the rather professional result.

"I'm sure they still pull, Octavia," Rosie said. "You can't *not* pull. They probably call it something American, like, erm . . . actually, I don't know. I'm sure they must do it though." She started doing her fingernails in clear gloss. "Yes, I've seen them do it on television and in films."

"I've got it. Why don't you ask Salah what the American word for pulling is and then you can suggest he do that word to me."

Rosie laughed but not in a completely enthusiastic way. More like a "you're a genius but that doesn't mean I'm cooperating," annoying way that made me take another unflattering snap of her.

She snatched my mobile and deleted the photo. "You don't think that will be too subtle?" she asked.

"You can't afford to be subtle with boys," I reminded her.

"Well, I have brothers, remember, and I don't think Salah is the sort of boy who likes to be shoved," she mused. It was an annoyingly good point. As shy as Rosie is, having grown up with four brothers, she knows loads about how boys work. She's always sharing handy tips with me on what boys *really* mean, and what they *really* think.

"Rosie, it's not about whether he likes being shoved or not, it's reassuring him that I *like* him. Anyway, take a shot of me," I insisted, passing her my phone. "All this Egyptian-ishness is making me feel too Cleopatra for words."

After Rosie had taken a few shots of me in different poses, Perdie and Artimis charged into our cabin. "Darlings!" they cried breathlessly. "The boys have just invaded our room!"

It was just the thing I had been hoping for. "Oh, how fabulous! Rosie and I were worried the Americans would be all awkward and intimidated by us."

"Which boys came into your room?" Rosie asked with surprising interest.

"Astin and Yo!" Perdie and Artimis squealed, jumping all over the room. "You know, Astin's the one with the squaddie haircut, and Yo's the big guy with the funny VR visor," Perdie added dreamily.

"Yar and he let us have a go of his visor thing. It was so cool," Artimis added.

"It was amazing. We went into King Tut's tomb and struggled with mummies and everything," Perdie explained excitedly.

"That's cool," Rosie agreed, relaxing back on her bed.

"They're still in there," Perdie added. "Come and see them? They're only wearing towels!"

I looked at Rosie and Rosie looked at me. "Boys in *towels*? Take us to them!" I demanded, and we charged off without bothering to dress.

Sometimes I find keeping up my over-the-top banter with boys a bit exhausting. But like so many other aspects of my character, it does the necessary job of hiding how poor I am. By acting madder-than-mad, everyone just presumes I'm eccentrically rich. And once they've assumed, I feel I can't let them down or they'll feel I misled them intentionally. Which, of course, I have. Really, being a teenager is terribly complicated, isn't it?

All the cabins on the boat were the same. They were furnished in a clean, modern Egyptian style, the main feature being the two large windows, which offered up a spectacular view of the Nile. There were two single beds, a chaise longue, a desk and chair, and a tiny en suite. The two boys—in white towels as promised—were stretched out on each of the girls' beds. They looked like two Mark Antonies.

Perdie sat on the bed with Yo, who was like a giant in the room even when he was sprawled on a bed. She snuggled closer to him.

Yo said, "Yo!" and put aside his VR visor. He was actually really handsome, which wasn't something I'd noticed under all his techno paraphernalia.

"What's up," Astin said—more as an announcement than a question. He was fit, in an overly manicured and pressed kind of way. Normally I'd want to muss a boy like him about, but I was too knocked out by the heat, so I snuggled up to him. Artimis was giving me a warning look, so I winked to reassure her she had nothing to worry about. I had other prey on my mind. I was just putting on a performance that I knew would get back to Salah—and hopefully make him get his skates on in the pulling department.

"You do realize," I scolded Astin, "that the gorgeous creatures who inhabit this room are my dearest friends."

"You do realize I'm in a towel," Astin pointed out in the most despairing attempt at an English accent. I didn't want to indulge him and endure the entire cruise with Americans taking the piss out of the way we spoke. Even though we do it to them all the time. "Darling, don't speak like that, it's tres, tres nonamusing," I chided.

Rosie laughed.

"Sorry, I was just screwing around." And then he made his eyebrows dance.

I love a boy who can make a fool of himself. Not that I'd ever pull that sort of boy, but I think it shows a certain amount of self-confidence. "Now, back to my point, my American friend from across the Atlantic. I do hope your intentions are dishonorable. Otherwise I shall be very severe with you and perhaps even speak to Carol."

"Totally dishonorable," Astin reassured me.

I eased myself away from him and sat by Yo. A girl

should never show too much attention to any one boy for too long. "And what about you, Yo? Are your intentions disreputable?"

"You're awesome, you know that?" he replied.

"Darling, of course I know that. I know that and much, much more. Now, to your friends, Sam and Salah, pray tell, where do their intentions lie?" I asked as if I didn't really, really *desperately* care.

"Sam is as dishonorable a guy as you'll find," Yo assured me proudly. "And Salah?" He looked to Astin.

"Only when it suits him," Yo said.

I arched a brow. "And does *moi* suit him, do you think?" I asked, expressing my marked disinterest this time by blowing on my toenails.

"I don't think there's a guy alive you wouldn't suit," he told me.

Charming but not the hoped-for confirmation that Salah was smitten to the point of illness with me. Still, they thought I was awesome, that should filter back to Salah. My work here was done. "Well, loving and leaving, darlings. I'm off to sun worship before tonight's belly dancing. Shall we all meet here for a few drinks before going up for dinner?" I asked the room.

"Definitely," Artimis replied, her baby-blue eyes still glued to Astin in a scarily worshipful way. "Astin's nicked a bottle of Sharazad!" she boasted, holding up a bottle of the local white wine. It looked less than promising. One of the upsides of living in my crumbly mansh with its lack of heating and leaking roof and moldy furniture is the ancient cellar, which can always be relied upon for a choice vintage wine. Papa hasn't caught on to my little business of selling off the really, really good stuff at auction. It was Mumsy's idea but she didn't know how to go about it, so I take a bottle to Sotheby's every so often and we split the profits. Occasionally I don't get that far and I end up drinking it with my mate-age. It's been tres, tres educational.

. . .

Rosie and I had been stretched out on the upper deck in our bikinis for a while and I was just about to drop off when I overheard Salah and Sam talking on the downstairs deck.

SAM: So, seriously, who's going for the Goddess?
SALAH: That'd be me. She likes the way I speak the language, remember?

The way I speak the language. What on earth could that mean? And then I realized, of course, he must be talking about "the language" of fine tailoring.

SAM: Okay, very funny. Yeah, you definitely made an impression there, but seriously, I can go for her, right?
SALAH: Yeah sure, you go for Octavia. Be my guest.

I swear I was so not being vain in assuming that *I* was the Goddess. Not that I was pleased that I was being passed along like a parcel. Bloody Sam, staking a claim on me when Salah fancied me!

After my heart stopped pounding, I nudged Rosie awake and told her that the Salah situation was now officially a red-alert crisis.

"What?" she mumbled drowsily.

"The boys. You need to shuffle them, Rosie!" I hissed. "Salah's given *Sam* the green light on *me*." Then I told her word for word what I'd overheard.

"So now you see what a mess this all is!"

"Not really. Sam likes you. Sam's fit. He's really nice. He's funny."

"I'm not after funny, darling. You know I don't date funny. Funny isn't sexy. The point is, as nice and fit and funny as Sam may be, he is *not* Salah."

"No," she agreed. "He's *not* Salah."

"There's clearly been a misunderstanding. I mean, look, I've got a plan, why don't you have Sam?"

"Well, that's charming!"

"What?"

"You're passing Sam along like a parcel now. And *me* for that matter."

"Sorry, I didn't mean it like that. It just sounded as if you really liked him, that's all. You do like him, don't you?"

"Yes, I like him but . . ."

"See? So that's perfect. Now can you pretty please go and explain to Salah that I quite fancy him."

"No! Octavia, you know I can't. It's just too weird. Anyway, think about it for a minute. If Salah *really* liked you, why doesn't he just go for you? It sounds to me like *he*'s the one passing you along to his mate." Then she stood up and left me on my own before I could think of a comeback.

Not that I could think of a suitable comeback. I felt suddenly cold with fear as I went over the conversation in my head and realized Rosie was completely right.

. . .

Rosie and I never made it to Artimis and Perdie's room for a glass of Sharazad because we were too busy working out what to do with the Salah situation. I'd decided I was still going to go for him even though he was very bad to tell Sam he could go for me. Then again, maybe I hadn't been clear about how much I liked him. I explained this to Rosie. "I have been flirting rather terribly with all the boys, so it isn't really his fault he got the wrong idea."

Rosie shrugged. As I came up with strategy after strategy—all of which Rosie shot down in flames—we snacked on some hellishly ancient vintage from my parents' ever-diminishing cellar, and a jar of caviar, which someone had given us for Christmas.

"Can you imagine? The thought of my parents eating

caviar, darling. Papa's taste buds run no further than overcooked meat and soggy puddings. Mumsy's not much better."

We had to scoop out the black eggs and eat them with our fingers. It was all quite a lot of fun and so I just blurted out, "Isn't it perfect that we never quarrel about boys, Rosie? I couldn't bear that. I mean, I'm sorry I'm obsessing about Salah, but I just don't understand what I could have done to give him the impression I wasn't interested in him."

Rosie gave me a cuddle. "Oh, Octavia. I'm sure it's nothing you've done. Maybe, erm, well, is it possible that even though he thinks you're hot, you're not, erm . . . his, erm . . . type?"

I grabbed at my heart in shock. "Darling! You heard Astin, I'm everyone's type!"

Rosie rolled her big cherub eyes and smiled. "You *do* know you're mad, right?"

Of course I knew I was mad, but still, I was beginning to get annoyed by the way she kept saying it all the time.

As I walked up the stairs in my Manolos (a gift from Rosie) I realized I might be slightly more tipsy than I thought, but then maybe a bit of Dutch courage was what was needed in a situation like this. After my bottle of Chateau Margeaux, Rosie had broken out the vodka. We'd only had a tiny taste to go with the caviar but while she was in the bathroom getting ready, I took a few extra mouthfuls. I'd overdone it slightly. We arrived late for dinner and ended up being seated alone.

I opened a menu describing exotic Arabic delicacies I'd never heard of. The waiters were carrying platters piled with spicy aromatic dishes. It was an intoxicating feast of colors and aromas.

The teachers were all at their own table, which was awash with bottles of wine. Yes, a civilizing drink was what we needed, I decided as I called to the waiter, who had a helpful little name tag attached to his dinner jacket.

"Could we see the wine list, Adel, please?" I asked. But he said—and this is true—"No!"

"What do you mean, 'no'?" I asked him, standing up from my chair. "Are you refusing to serve me?" But he walked away from our table, his face as impassive as a temple statue.

I complained to Rosie, who was gazing off in the middle distance. I followed her gaze and that's when I saw that hungry, boy-longing look on her face. Sam was at the opposite end of the room seated with Salah, Astin, Yo, Artimis, and Perdie. So there it was. Now I had the proof. She did fancy Sam!

"I knew it, darling."

"Knew what?" she asked.

"You *do* fancy Sam, see!" I pointed over at Sam, only I may have spoken a bit too loudly.

"Shhh!" Rosie shushed me crossly. "Octavia, are you *drunk*?"

"No!" I insisted. "Well, I don't know. I might be a bit squiffy. I took a shot or two of Dutch Courage while you were getting ready."

Rosie put her head in her hands and groaned.

CHAPTER 7

❣ SALAH ❣

*For the first time in my life, I wanted something from someone
else. Worse than that, I wanted something that I wasn't
one hundred percent certain I could have.*

After dinner we were ushered upstairs to the bar for a Dervish dancing demonstration. Octavia was totally wasted. And not in a fun way. Sam wanted to do something about the situation before she got busted and sent home. If the teachers weren't so drunk themselves they'd have noticed her lurching around the room—but then maybe they were used to lurching because of Yo and his visor.

Mohammed, still dressed as Indiana Jones, was attempting to read his speech about the dance program. He was fighting off interruptions from the teachers.

Reading from his note cards he explained, "The dance of the Dervish has been performed for over seven hundred years. It is the dance of the Sufi."

"They're a mystical order of Islam, aren't they?" piped up Carol.

"And they go into a kind of trance state," added Nigel.

"I wish Nigel would go into a trance state," Octavia stage-whispered, and everyone muffled laughter.

Rosie nudged her, which almost knocked her flying into Mohammed.

Mohammed looked flustered, like he'd lost his place. He shuffled his cards. "The dervish is chanting, '*la illaha illa'llah*' during his dance."

"Ah yes, 'there is no God, but God,'" Nigel added proudly, standing up like he was waiting for applause.

"Fantastic, Nigel. Fantastic!" Carol clapped her approval.

"Yes, brilliant, Nigel Octavia drawled." "We truly are in the presence of genius!"

Mohammed mopped some sweat from his brow and continued. "But you see, many of the dervish dancers prefer simply to say 'Allah' in the event they die while in their trance. Then the last word on their lips would be *Allah*."

"Well Allah to that!" Octavia declared and started clapping. She looked ridiculous but thankfully everyone was distracted by the lights, which were dramatically dimmed and the glass stage in the middle of the room was transformed into a kaleidoscope of lights. Dervish music pounded through the room. A tall guy dressed in a traditional dervish costume with a full skirt and tall hat stepped onto the dance floor and began to spin.

Octavia almost knocked him flying as she careened across the dance floor and pushed her way outside, onto the deck. Rosie chased after her.

I nudged Sam.

"I think we'd better check on your *goddess*."

"What's up?"

"She ran out to the deck. Rosie just went after her."

I'd planned to be the one to help Rosie, but Sam was out the door and onto the deck before me. The girls were leaning over the railing, looking at a boat moored next to us. Inside the top cabin of the boat, some kind of a disco seemed to be in progress.

"How are you traveling, my Queen of the Nile?" Sam asked Octavia. She was leaning over the side of the boat as if she was going to be sick. Rosie was rubbing her back supportively. I resisted an urge to rub Rosie's back.

"Oh, that's right, you won me in some game of craps or something, didn't you?"

Sam and I looked at one another. "I think she's drunk," I suggested quietly.

"We just came up for some air," Rosie explained, looking at me directly. "Octavia wasn't feeling very well."

"Come on, Goddess Octavia, let's take a walk around the deck," Sam said, taking her arm and putting it over his shoulder.

I looked at Octavia. She was even drunker than I had thought. I felt sort of sorry for her. She seemed to have everything going for her—looks, wealth, and popularity—and here she was, incapable of even focusing. She was a total mess.

"Sorry, I didn't mean to get so drunk," Octavia apologized, as if she knew what I was thinking.

"'Course not. Let's get moving," Sam said, gently supporting her as they began to walk around the deck.

I put my hand lightly on Rosie's back and steered her toward the comfy white deck sofas. "It's okay. Sam will look after her," I told her.

"She's not usually like this," Rosie explained.

"No?"

"Oh, what am I saying?" She sighed, dropping down beside me. "She's always like this," she admitted. "I don't mean drunk. I don't mean that. Of course not, but you know, she's always a bit out there."

I nodded, totally gripped by the sound of her voice and the closeness of her lips.

"She's always the center of attention. Which is good. I'm not jealous or anything because I'm completely shy and useless with new people and actually I prefer the shadows to the limelight but you know sometimes it can be exhausting. Sorry I'm babbling, which is something I usually never do. Well, not very much. Usually I'm the really quiet one. The girl no one notices."

"I noticed you," I told her quietly.

"Oh, I'm not complaining. Oh god, I am complaining, aren't I? How selfish. I mean, of course people *notice* me, otherwise they'd be bumping into me all the time, and yes, you did notice me. You listened to my music."

"How's it going? The piece you were working on," I asked. I wanted to keep her talking.

"The key change thing you suggested was just perfect. I meant to say thank you this evening, but then everything went all, well, pear shaped."

"Yeah, not exactly according to plan."

"No."

After that we sat in companionable silence looking up at the sky. This was my first night in Egypt in years, but as I looked up and saw the stars, I felt like I'd never been away. Even in the artificial Egypt of the *Nefertiti*, I felt like I was home.

"That's Osiris," I said, pointing up at the sky.

Rosie leaned back on the sofa, and her head rested on my arm. I took the finger of her right hand and guided her around the clear sky.

"Wow. We're actually looking at Osiris in Egypt. That's him, right? The one with the funny hat?"

I laughed. "That's the man. God of the underworld. He's the guy who judges the souls of the dead."

"And he married Isis. Mohammed told me that."

"That's the one. He married Isis. She's the one you see holding the ankh, with the moon in her hair," I explained.

"It's so glorious," she said with amazement. "I suddenly really feel like I'm in Egypt. I love how the stars seem so close I feel like we can just reach out and grab them."

"I know. You know the Bedouins can track their way across the desert with them."

"How envy making you are," she said, smiling at me.

"What do you mean?"

"You just know so much. But why wouldn't you! You are Egyptian and, oh, shut up, Rosie," she cried, slapping her hand over her mouth. Before I realized what I was doing, I reached out and pulled her hand away.

"No, don't stop," I told her, smiling.

"But I'm babbling again. My brothers are always telling me to shut up."

"I'm not telling you to shut up. I'm telling you *not* to shut up," I insisted. "And for the record, I miss seeing the night sky too. We don't have stars in New York. Well, not these kinds of stars."

"I much prefer these stars," she said quietly, after a pause.

"Me too," I replied.

"Do you miss Egypt? I'm sure I would. If I came from here, that is. Not that I have a clue. This is my first time and I'm just seeing it as a tourist, but I love the feel of it and the liveliness of it. I even love Mohammed, don't you? He's so cool. Did you know he went to Oxford?"

"I imagine there's a lot more to him than meets the eye. He's an interesting guy."

Suddenly Octavia landed beside me. I looked around for Sam but he'd disappeared.

"They look like they're having fun," Octavia announced, pointing to the boat moored next to ours. There was a group of older people dancing, having the time of their lives.

"Yeah they do," I agreed, though I was focusing beyond the boat to the shore, where there was a different kind of activity going on. Brightly decorated horse-drawn caleches were taking tourists around Luxor, street vendors were selling souvenirs, and outdoor cafes were buzzing with domino-playing locals.

"Unlike this boring lot here," Octavia groaned. "Hardly party central on the good ship *Nefertiti* tonight, is it?"

"I'm enjoying the quiet. It clears my head," Rosie told her.

"What a fibber. I bet you're composing something and your head is as noisy as an orchestra," Octavia told her, reaching over my lap to take Rosie's hand and give it a squeeze.

I felt a surge of irritation that she was close enough to

Rosie to touch her and pissed that she'd had to lean over my lap to do it. I was relieved when Sam turned up breathless with a bottle of water. He pulled Octavia up. "Come on, Octavia, let's keep walking, and look, I've got you something to drink."

"Oh no, I don't want any more to drink," she groaned.

"It's okay, it's water," he reassured her.

"I'm so horrendously drunk, aren't I?" she said to everyone and no one. "You must all hate me."

"No one hates *you*," Sam promised. "Besides, no ones really noticed. Carol is totally wasted. Did you see her flirting with that Nigel guy?"

"Dear Nigel. At least someone's pulling." Octavia murmured.

Sam looked confused. He shrugged. "The dervish dancer's started. Wanna go inside and check it out, Octavia?"

"You go, darling. I wouldn't want you to miss that for the world, Sam."

Sam looked at me with one of his, I'm-drowning-here-man-what-do-I-do? looks.

"Yeah, he looks kind of cool, Rosie. Want to come check him out?" I suggested.

Rosie opened her mouth to reply.

"No," Octavia snapped.

"So what do you say, Rosie?" I asked, pretending

I hadn't heard Octavia's objection. "Sam can hang out with Octavia."

Rosie replied, "I'd actually quite like to . . ."

I wasn't sure how to play this, but I figured that given how drunk Octavia was, maybe, just maybe, I could maneuver Rosie downstairs and leave Sam to Octavia.

And then Sam threw me a life preserver. "Yeah, Octavia needs some more air. You guys go ahead. We'll be down in a bit."

We went inside where the lights were low and the dervish dancer was spinning around in the center of the room. We stood at the back and Rosie had to shout in my ear to be heard above the noise of the music. "It's just that she overheard you discuss her with Sam, and she's pretty upset about it."

I wondered nervously what it was Octavia had heard and then I remembered Sam asking me for the green light on Octavia. "Do you think she likes Sam?" I asked, trying not to sound too hopeful.

Rosie giggled and then said, "God, I would be sick if I spun around like that." She pointed to the dancer who had been spinning around and around without stopping for over ten minutes. "I used to love making myself dizzy when I was little," she added.

I smiled, imagining her as a little girl, her long strawberry-blond curls whirling about like the dervish dancer's skirts. I took the opportunity to drape my arm loosely around her as I leaned in to reply. But then as I smelled her hair my mind went blank and I couldn't think of anything to say. I just wanted to kiss her. In the end I managed to shout, "No, you'd be a natural." But I don't think she heard.

She clapped her hands along with everyone else.

"I'm really looking forward to the belly dancing," she said a moment later. "It sounds really cool. Not that I'd ever do something like that."

More than anything I wanted to put my lips on her bow-shaped mouth, but I felt too nervous to kiss her, she was too, too . . .

Too ethereal.

After a while Rosie shouted in my ear, "Octavia wants you to know she likes you. That was why she was upset by your conversation. She heard you telling Sam he could have her."

I took a breath and thought about it. "Yeah, that would suck. I'm sorry about that."

"She thinks she's given you the wrong impression. Sort of, you know, made you think she doesn't fancy you. She can do that sometimes."

"It's nothing like that," I assured her. "I think she's hilarious, but I'm interested in someone else," I shouted.

I watched her bite her lip like a little girl and look away. "Octavia can have any boy she wants."

Again I was stuck for what to say. I didn't want to

waste this opportunity to be alone with Rosie, so I just pulled her closer and pretended I hadn't heard what she'd said.

"All the boys prefer Octavia," Rosie continued, "even when they pretend not to. I mean, I don't blame them. She's much prettier than me. Not to mention more exotic!"

"I don't know if that's true," I told her.

"It is," she insisted. "I'm shy and ordinary and Octavia is, well, look at her! It's just no fun being second best all the time. Do you know what I mean?"

"I don't see why you should feel that way. For what it's worth, I think you're way prettier than Octavia."

She bit her lip again. "Octavia's not pretty, she's stunning."

I wanted to say something remarkable then, something that would make Rosie look up into my eyes and see what I saw—that not only was she incredibly talented but she was gorgeous; an angel whose big golden eyes warmed my soul. I wanted to kiss her and reassure her that she wasn't second best. She was most definitely the Best. Gorgeous, and more important, real.

In that second as the music stopped and the lights went on, I realized that for the first time in my life I wanted something from someone else. Worse than that, I wanted something that I wasn't one-hundred-percent certain I could have.

Everyone was clapping and cheering. I looked over and caught Yo making out with Perdita in one of the corner booths. Lucky bastard. Even Carol and Nigel were gazing longingly into one another's eyes.

Mohammed stepped forward again armed with his note. "And now we are proud to present the beautiful Sorayah. The Egyptian belly dance is the most ancient of all surviving dances. It tells the story of a woman's life; her spiritual life, her loves, her longings and losses. It is a prayer to her family and a celebration of life. I ask each of you to hold your hands out and express gentleness in your own way."

"Oh no!" cried one of the girls, and Rosie and I both laughed.

Mohammed clapped enthusiastically as the belly dancer skipped into the bar in her sparkling costume, her long black tresses flowing down her back. "You let the music move through you. Many peoples of the Arab world perform this dance, but it is from Egypt they learn the language. We are a proud and ancient people. There is a saying, Egyptian belly dancers glisten, other belly dancers sweat." He laughed at his little joke. "Enough now," he insisted, taking off his hat. "Let us clap our hands and celebrate the glistening Sorayah."

Sorayah was standing on the brightly lit glass dance floor. The overhead lights dimmed, the music began, and cheers went up from the jocks as she wriggled and swayed her spangled hips hypnotically. It was a sight to behold, but not for long because that was when Rosie put her arm through mine and looked into my eyes for the very first time. "God, she's really good, isn't she?" she asked.

But I didn't get to revel in the shock of her skin against mine or the look she'd given me, because just then Sam charged in. He grabbed me and insisted, "Quick, Salah, you've got to help. Octavia climbed onto the other boat."

"She what?" Rosie asked, removing her arm from mine.

"Just hurry up! She totally lost it. I couldn't stop her, dude."

"How did she make it over there?" I asked Sam angrily as the three of us made our way out to the dock. "That boat's railing is over six feet away."

"She made me help her."

"What?" Rosie shrieked.

"Rosie, why don't you go back inside and make sure none of the teachers come out," I told her, taking control. "The last thing we need is one of them busting us."

"But what about Octavia?"

"I'll go and bring her back," I assured her.

Sam argued, "I can get her, I just need a hand."

"No you'd better leave it to me," I insisted. "If there's a problem with the other boat, I speak Arabic. The last thing we want is a security problem, or worse, for the police to get involved." *Believe me, I don't want to be the one to rescue her,* I wanted to add but didn't.

"Promise you won't be mean to her," Rosie begged.

"I promise." I was so going to wring Octavia's neck. "Just go and keep the teachers inside."

When Rosie was out of earshot, I turned to Sam. "What the hell were you thinking, helping her climb onto the other boat?"

"Okay, I know it was dumb, but the girl's *amazing*. She was goofing around. She kept daring me to do all this crazy stuff and I kept saying no but eventually, well, I felt like this chicken, so I agreed to help her over the railings."

I shook my head in disbelief.

"I thought I'd join her, but once she was over there"—he pointed to some figures visible through the window—"she went straight in and started dancing like a maniac. If any of the teachers see that, she'll be sent back to London."

I looked in at the crowd inside. It didn't take long to spot Octavia dancing while a crowd of elderly people clapped and cheered.

"Okay, wait here and pray we don't get busted. I'll need your help to get her back."

"Sure. And Salah. Thanks. I owe you big-time."

"Don't you always?" I said, tossing him my suit jacket. I climbed over the railing and jumped across to the other boat.

Octavia's audience wasn't about to let me get near her. They'd formed a circle around her and were clapping in time to some fifties music as she writhed around the dance floor like a demented gazelle. It wasn't very goddesslike.

"Excuse me, ladies and gentlemen," I called as I grabbed Octavia. "Show's over. The performer has another engagement elsewhere."

"Aw shucks, fella. We was enjoying the show," an old guy in a cowboy hat and a walker told me.

"I'm sure you were," I said as I led Octavia through the crowd.

"Salah?" Octavia asked when the fresh air hit her. I could smell the wine on her breath. "You came." She smiled.

"Looks like it. This really isn't cool, Octavia. They could have called security if someone had reported a strange guy climbing onto the boat."

"But you're not strange."

The old folks had followed us out onto the deck, so I shut up.

"You take care of that girl there," the Texan warned, tottering ahead of the group, the rubber wheels of his walker squeaking. "She's a pretty little thing. One in a million. We haven't had so much fun since . . ."

"Oh, he will," Octavia called out, then added in a southern accent, "Y'all take care now!" She waved and they clapped their approval. She wouldn't walk, so I finally had to lift her up and carry her over to Sam and that was when she put her arms around my neck. I was about to say something when she kissed me.

I pulled away but the damage was done. I looked across the railing at Sam and watched his face go cold. And it got worse. Carol and Nigel were behind him. I probably should have been worried about expulsion or getting sent back to New York or a million other things that could change the course of my life. But Rosie was there, too, and all I could think of as I saw the look of agony slash across her face was how much I wanted to throttle Octavia, and I'm not even a throttling sort of guy. At least I never thought I was.

And don't give me the lecture Sam gave me later. I was there, and it is a hell of a lot harder than you might imagine to push a girl off you when she's got her arms wrapped around your neck and her tongue halfway down your throat.

But my protestations seemed weak even to me.

CHAPTER 8

··♥ ROSIE ♥··

*It only took one sentence, and like a pharaoh's curse,
all hope was dashed.*

I was rooted to the spot, rendered as stonelike as the Sphinx by what I'd seen.

"What on earth were you doing on that boat?" Nigel demanded.

The passengers on the other boat were still waving and cheering loudly to Octavia. Salah passed Octavia to Sam and then athletically jumped over to the *Nefertiti* himself. He was annoyingly fit despite being the most hateful boy in the world.

Bloody Octavia and bloody Salah! At least Octavia was drunk and she was also, well, Octavia. Besides, I knew she fancied Salah, so I couldn't really be surprised by her behavior. It was Salah I hated for having deceived me earlier in the evening with all that rubbish about fancying someone else more than Octavia. And I hated myself even more for being so sad and stupid to have thought he meant me.

Most of all, I was disappointed in him for being like every other boy in the entire world who claims to fancy this girl or that when really all he really wants is to pull Octavia.

"I don't think she's as cute as you." He'd actually said that. The liar! He'd almost made me believe he thought I was prettier than the most beautiful girl in the world! The madness of it all didn't make it less galling. What had Sam called her, a goddess? How is any girl supposed to compete with a goddess?

"Oh, do stop going on," Octavia chided Nigel. "I'm sure Carol would rather be whisked off her feet to trip the light fantastic than listen to you berate a spirited girl like moi who was merely having a little fun."

As if on cue, the pensioners opposite called out, "Bye, Octavia. Thanks for the show!"

She had the world at her feet.

Octavia waved back and blew kisses.

"And what have you got to say for yourself, Salah?" Carol asked sternly. Even so, I spotted a look pass between Carol and Nigel and knew at once that Octavia was going to get away with it *again*. A really, really mean part of me would have quite liked to see her gated. Only then she'd be upset and I'd probably end up feeling sorry for her.

Salah was looking at me as he replied, "Well, I didn't think it would be safe to let her go alone, Carol."

And Sam quickly added, "They insisted she go and visit them. They wouldn't take no for an answer, would they Octavia?" He nudged her to agree.

"No's never much of an answer," Octavia replied, batting her ridiculously long lashes at Salah.

I could tell without looking that Salah was trying to make eye contact with me, but I wasn't having any of it. I still had a bit of pride left and I was clinging to it like a life jacket.

"Well, I must say, it's reassuring to see that Bowers produces such fine gentlemen," Nigel said, looking at Carol with sickening admiration.

"Oh Nigel," Carol twanged.

Right then I knew Octavia wasn't going to be gated. Nigel and Carol didn't want their trip spoiled although they said they didn't want to spoil *our* trip. Teachers are so two-faced like that.

Nigel, encouraged by her simpering, continued. "Though I can't say I'm surprised that a teacher of your caliber has produced such fine, thoughtful, polite young men, Carol. Bowers and these young boys' parents must count themselves as most fortunate to have their sons molded by your capable hands."

It was truly vomitsome.

Nigel seemed to realize that things were getting a bit inappropriate in the teacher-flirting department and composed himself. "Well, erm, that is to say (awkward cough), I think it's time for you young ones to get a bit of kip before tomorrow's excursion. Six a.m. wake-up call, remember!"

"Yes, sir . . . I mean, Nigel," Octavia agreed, saluting and then kneeling and bowing in a scraping, groveling sort of way, which made me laugh. This is what always happened with Octavia. She always made me laugh or did something really kind and I'd forgive her for being so outrageous.

"Off you go then," Carol added, practically shoving us off the deck and back into the now-empty bar so she could be alone with our tragic little teacher.

Salah and Sam did one of those sad, alpha-male hand-slapping rituals that ended with fiddly fingers and guffaws all round. At times like this, I really wonder why we are so entranced with boys.

"So, do you want to come to our cabin for a night-cap?" Sam asked, trying to regain some coolness as he finally remembered our existence.

"No," I replied firmly, glaring at Octavia. "We need some sleep. We've been up since five this morning."

Octavia laughed. "Oh don't be such a bore, darling. We're young! Sleep is for the elderly."

I glared at her. She was really annoying me.

"I'd like to get some sleep myself, actually," Salah added, looking pointedly at Sam. "See you guys in the morning," he said. I could feel his eyes searching for mine, but I wasn't going to give him the satisfaction. In fact, I planned never to look into his eyes again. I was immune to his charms. To prove this I began to hum as if I wasn't even aware of his presence, let alone his smoldering good looks. He could take his looks and his charm and drown them in the Nile for all I cared, and I really, really intended to mean that in every fiber of my being.

Octavia went to kiss him but Salah strode off straight past her toward the stairs. "See you at six then."

"Yeah, at six," Sam agreed, looking confused as he followed his friend.

Back in our cabin we found tomorrow's itinerary laid out on our turned-down beds. I was still humming away, having lost my humming inhibition halfway to our cabin. I'd worked myself into a lung-blasting noise by the time Octavia told me to shut up and hit me with her pillow.

I climbed into bed with a deep-seated case of the grumps.

Octavia didn't go to sleep straight away. Nor did she seem even mildly aware of my grumps. No, Octavia was babbling away happily, even as she cleaned her teeth. Over the sound of the running tap I caught words like "Salah" and "darling" and "hilarious" and "pull."

I put my pillow over my head to drown her out and howled "Shut up!" into my mattress.

"What a night, Rosie," Octavia said with a sigh as she finally climbed into her own bed. And then she started singing, "Oh, what a night!" I don't know where she digs up these horrible old songs, but I wished she'd bury them.

"Goodnight," I said through gritted teeth.

"What a magical Egyptian knight in shining armor Salah turned out to be. Thank you, thank you, thank you, darling Rosie, for being the bestest friend in the world. I knew you'd sort it all out so we could be together. You always do. You're such a brick."

A brick?

"A brick?"

I wish I *had* a brick, I thought. I'd hurl it at her. Instead I said, "Your hangover will hit you like a brick tomorrow and we have to be up at six."

"Oh, I'll be up and raring to go. I can't wait to play hide-and-seek in the tombs with Salah. I bet there'll be all sorts of romantic nooks and crannies for pulling."

Then she climbed out of her bed and gave me a cuddle. "I really do love you, Rosie, you know that, don't you?"

"Yes," I said, trying not to stay cross.

"I don't know what you said to Salah, but it must have worked."

I wanted to scream, "Why do you have to have *every* boy? I wanted Salah. I thought he wanted me. And he might have if you hadn't set your sights on him. No boy can resist you and I hate you." But, of course, I didn't say any of that because I didn't have the guts. All I said was, "Not a problem. Go to sleep now."

Octavia climbed back into her own bed. "You're right about Sam by the way," she sighed, nuzzling into the Egyptian cotton of her sheets. "I think he's adorable. I saw you from the boat. You two look great together."

A sudden idea occurred to me. "I know, why don't *you* pretend to like Sam? I bet that would really make Salah jealous."

Octavia looked thoughtful. "Really? You wouldn't mind me doing that?"

"No. Go right ahead," I insisted as I lay there wondering if there wasn't still a microscopic chance that if she spent enough time *pretending* to like Sam she might actually realize she really did like Sam. Which would leave Salah . . . then she said the words that sealed the tomb on my hope.

"Isn't it so, so perfect that we're not the sort of girls who fight over boys, darling?"

I couldn't even answer I felt so ill. And more than a little bit two-faced.

⊚

Tuesday, Day 2
Nefertiti sails to Esna

Sunrise: 06:24 Sunset: 17:57
06:00 Wake-up call

06:30–07:00 Breakfast in the Nefertiti restaurant

07:00 Visit the West Bank by bus

12:00 *Nefertiti* sails to Esna

13:00 Lunch in the Nefertiti restaurant

17:00 Teatime on the lower deck

20:00 Cocktail & presentation in the Ankh bar
Dress code: Elegant attire

20:30 Dinner in the Nefertiti restaurant

22:00 Nubian show in the Ankh bar

23:00 DVD in suites: *Death on the Nile*

Overnight in Esna

CHAPTER 9

❤❤❤ SAM ❤❤❤

Every man for himself!

Salah and I bumped into Yo, Astin, Artimis, and Perdie on our way down to our cabin. They invited us in for a drink even though it was clear they wanted to be alone. You could almost hear them muttering under their breath, "Please say no, please say no."

So I said, "sounds great!" just to jerk them around. Salah didn't even stop to say hi. As if he was the one with a gripe. If anyone had a reason to be pissed, it was me. And after a couple of glasses of the local vino, I was prepared to set the record straight.

I headed back to our room, figuring he'd have some big apology prepared. But he was in bed, reading.

"You're a real jerk, you know that?" I told him, flinging down his stupid suit jacket, which I'd hung on to for some reason.

He looked away from his book and held my gaze. "Believe me, I didn't want the whole kiss thing." The way he spoke in a totally calm way when I was burning up inside made me even angrier.

"Yeah? Well, it didn't look like that to me. Or to anyone else."

"As if I had a choice. I *did* pull away."

"Yo and Astin didn't think you did." Which was a straight-out lie, but I continued anyway. " *'Oh, I speak the language.'* They were *Texans*! Since when do you need Arabic to speak to Texans?"

He held my gaze for a beat as if weighing what I'd said—and deeming it unworthy of a reply, he turned back to his book.

That fueled my anger even more, so I turned off the light, plunging the room into darkness even though I wasn't remotely ready for bed. I stood there for a minute, feeling like a total loser, unable to see where my bed was. Eventually Salah turned on his reading lamp. "Sure you don't need some light?"

That really pissed me off—his cool attitude. How dare he just act like nothing was wrong after kissing *my* girl! "I'm fine, thanks," I told him sarcastically.

He shrugged. "Whatever."

"Yeah, whatever," I repeated. Whatever that meant. He was making me feel like I was the jerk. I felt like storming out of the room, but the rest of the boat was either partying in their cabins or sound asleep. I had no choice but to go to bed.

. . .

I honestly didn't expect to see Octavia at six the next morning. I figured she would still be sprawled in bed, her head hammering away with Nubian drums like any respectable Manhattan princess who'd consumed cheap wine on an empty stomach. But there she was at six a.m., more glorious than any creature I had ever seen. She walked in, arm in arm with Rosie. Rosie looked about as miserable as I felt.

Not only was Octavia looking happy, but she was dressed for a night of clubbing in killer heels, jeans, and a white strappy camisole. I swear to God you could not avoid noticing Octavia. She was something else. She was also holding a big lime-green hat and Jackie O sunglasses. It was definitely not your average hangover outfit.

Rosie looked great too, in orange capri pants and a black lace top, with an orange bikini peeking through. I watched Salah's eyes as the girls bounced over to us—searching for who he was checking out, but he didn't so much as glance at them. He kept on reading the stupid Egyptian newspaper he'd got off Mohammed, even though he admitted he was struggling with the Arabic.

Rosie was wearing an orange straw cowboy hat and big black sunglasses. Her shoes were even higher than Octavia's but not as dainty.

"Morning, darlings!" Octavia breezed, air kissing first me, and then Salah. "Isn't it a *perfect* day?"

I pointed out that it was, in fact, still dark. The Elderly boat, which had been moored alongside us the night before, had departed. We could just see the sun beginning to glow on the horizon.

"Oh but it's a beautiful desert dark, darling, so evocative, so romantic. Aren't you madly excited about our trip to the Valley of the Kings and Queens?" she asked, plonking down beside Salah and flooding my nostrils with a faint scent of something intoxicating. Something I never wanted to stop smelling. "Loving the shirt, Sam," she added, lightly pulling on my collar.

"Thanks," I said, pathetically grateful she'd deigned to touch me.

Rosie had already gone off to grab some food. It was just a few minutes after six and most people weren't up yet. Mohammed was sitting at the teachers' table with Mr. Bell and Ms. Doyle. There was no sign of Carol and Nigel.

"Doesn't Mohammed look all forlorn over there at the teacher's table? Like a little boy being punished for something he didn't do," Octavia remarked. "I really think we should try and bring him over to our side, Sam, don't you? What do you think, darling?" she asked, nudging Salah.

"Go for it," Salah replied without looking up from

his paper. I swear to God he was being deliberately cool. I kicked him under the table. "Yes, *darling*, what do you think?" I asked him, hoping to get some sort of rise from him.

He looked up. "Huh?"

"Octavia thinks we should kidnap Mohammed and show him a good time."

Salah looked over at Mohammed, who was morosely drinking his thick Arabic coffee. "I think that *is* Mohammed's way of having a good time," he reflected before returning his attention to his paper.

I looked at Octavia and rolled my eyes meaningfully, but she was looking at Rosie, who was returning from the buffet. "What did you get me?" Octavia asked, peering excitedly at Rosie's plate.

"I thought you'd get your own," Rosie replied flatly as she sat down next to me.

"Rosie, you are funny sometimes."

"What do you want? I'll go up for you," I offered, seeing my chance to shine, even if it was in a blatantly suck-up way. "Pastries? Eggs?"

"Oh, darling, *everything*. Just pile it on," she said, gesturing with her hands. "I'm famished. Oh, and can you have them make me an espresso? I'll simply die if I don't have my morning espresso. This coffee . . . ," she added, pointing at the pot on the table as if it were a pot of sewage, "it's just so wrong." Then she shivered as if even being in its presence were a form of torture.

"I'll move it," I suggested, but Salah placed his hand over mine as I reached over to grab the irksome matter. "I like it," he said, looking straight at Octavia. What was his problem? One minute the guy's telling me he isn't interested in Octavia, then he goes and tongues her, then he acts all confrontational.

As I rose from the table, Rosie looked at me and rolled her eyes. "You do realize she's completely mad, right?"

"I wish you wouldn't keep saying that, darling. It's getting tired," Octavia groaned, laying herself across the table.

"See!" Rosie said, pointing at Octavia's face, which was now flattened on the table. "This is not how sane people behave. She's completely crazy."

"That's okay," I told her. "Ask Salah, I love crazy," I told her truthfully, because it was partly Octavia's totally wild behavior that turned me on so much. She dared to be at odds with the mainstream. It occurred to me that I was even prepared to forgive her flirting with Salah. If anything, last night had made me determined to do whatever it took to make her mine. I stood up to go to the buffet.

"I'll join you," called Rosie, rushing out of her chair.

"It's okay, I can handle it," I told her.

"No. I don't think you can," she told me in a weirdly

significant way. And as her hand brushed mine as we both reached for the eggs, I wondered if *she* might be flirting with me.

"Tell you what. You probably know better than me what she likes," I said, and turned back for the table.

When Rosie returned with Octavia's breakfast, she glared at me. I was definitely going to be avoiding eye contact with her from now on. I so didn't need any more complications on this trip. No, I'd keep my focus on Octavia and her needs.

Her needs included her request—before we boarded the bus—to carry her backpack containing two gallons of water and a ton of makeup.

"Not a problem," I insisted.

"Can you take Rosie's stuff as well, Sam?"

"Sure, why not?" I agreed, slinging the extra load over my other shoulder. Rosie started to tell me it wasn't necessary, but I cut her off and snatched the bag from her.

Nigel and Carol eventually surfaced, looking worse for wear. As we were boarding the bus, they fumbled around, feeding each other painkillers, still wearing the same clothes from the night before. Mr. Bell and Ms. Doyle exchanged significant looks. The rest of us busted out laughing. You had to see it, but I swear to God, imagining puny little Nigel and Carol together was beyond hilarious.

Octavia nudged Nigel and called him an "old dog."

He was apparently too paralyzed by his hangover or embarrassment to respond.

In the end, we didn't get going until 7:30. Despite my maneuvering, I'd ended up beside Rosie and Octavia was in the window seat beside Salah. Mohammed stood at the front with his mic.

"You really don't need to carry my stuff," Rosie started up again, but I shushed her to listen to Mohammed. "So America and England, hope you are well this morning. I want to give you some blah, blah, blah about the Egyptian peoples but first I like to say, God Save the Queen and Yankee Doodle Dandy. And I will warn you about some bad people you will find at the Valley of the Kings!" He shook his finger at us in warning. "These men they will try to give you gifts."

"Oh, how lovely!" exclaimed Octavia, clapping her hands.

"No, not lovely," Mohammed warned her sternly. "You know what you do with these gifts?"

"Treasure them," Octavia said firmly. "Oh, and say . . . what's that word for 'thank you,' Salah?"

"*Shookron*," he said flatly.

"*Shookron*?" Mohammed echoed. "No! You don't thank these people. You throw their gifts on the ground," Mohammed insisted angrily, demonstrating with one arm the force involved.

I was watching the way Octavia teased Mohammed,

ignoring Salah and Rosie, who were looking out the window at the traffic of sad donkeys pulling carts of vegetables; women draped in black, carrying jugs and even boxes on their heads; and the usual stream of caleches, trucks, and cars. I took a few shots of the scene—mainly out of habit. I hadn't even checked my shutter speed.

"I assure you, Octavia, it is not rude," Mohammed continued. "These men, they give you scarf, scarabee, T-shirt. They say, 'For you welcome to Egypt, I am your friend, where are you from, my friend? You are my sister. Take this gift, no charge for you.' But then after you return from the Valley of the Kings. They catch you!" he raged, eyes glinting as he made a melodramatic grabbing gesture. "And they say, 'Where's my money?' They say, 'Give me bloody fifty pounds sterling for that scarf.' They are not good peoples. No, they are bad peoples. If you want these things you can ask me and I can take you to the shop and get the good price."

"Well, I think the Egyptians are simply lovely!" Octavia exclaimed, clasping her hands to her heart theatrically. She touched Salah as she said this, but he didn't turn around.

"Thank you, Octavia." Mohammed bowed. "Yes, we are lovely people. But not all. Even in England and America, you have some bad men I am thinking."

Normally it was Nigel and Carol's job to interrupt Mohammed, but they were snoring in the back of the bus, as were Old Man Bell and Doyle. Everyone else was cracking up at the banter between Octavia and Mohammed. Even Yo was laughing under his visor. Although it could have just been because he had beheaded a mummy with his virtual chainsaw—it's hard to tell with Yo.

Salah and Rosie were both stone-faced.

"Now, after the boat across the Nile, we see the funeral mortuary temple of the Queen Hatshepsut," Mohamed explained.

"Oooh, we love her," Octavia cried. "She wanted to build her father a big golden obelisk."

"The god Amun, yes, clever Octavia remembers. See, she pays attention," Mohammed praised, glaring at the teachers. "Hatshepsut is completely crazy queen. But she was the only ruling queen of Egypt and ruled for two decades." He held up two fingers so we could absorb this factoid.

"After she died, they destroy many inscriptions and statues of her. But still much is left. We will see this and after we go to visit three tombs. Not Tutankhamen because that is forty Egyptian pounds more and bloody rip-off. No, we see Rameses II and then we see tombs with smallest queues."

By the time we arrived at the boat, Octavia was asleep, her head on Salah's shoulder. He nudged her awake roughly and glared at me as if I'd done something wrong.

"What?" I asked, but he didn't reply.

After we disembarked, I asked Salah again, "What's up with you?"

But Mohammed interrupted. "Take your water! It's hot," he yelled.

He was right. It was insanely hot and there was me, carrying a lifetime supply of makeup, sunblock, and four gallons of water plus my camera gear and other essentials, including my Knicks hat. I hadn't put it on yet, figuring it might be wise not to broadcast my Americanism to the hustlers.

I was thankful for the breeze on the barge we took across the river. The vastness of Queen Hatshepsut's temple looked dramatic against the backdrop of the desert mountains. I got some great shots of the engine on the barge and some cool shots of feet. Salah looked miserable in his cream pinstripe suit. I couldn't believe he was wearing a jacket but then so were Mohammed and the other Egyptians. Some of them were even in big woolen sweaters. It might be 100 degrees but as Mohammed kept telling us, it was winter to them.

He was right about the gift-thrusting mafia too. They were all over us the moment we stepped foot on the west bank.

"Hello, my friend. England? God save the Queen!"

"American? Howdy pardner! Take this please my friend, my brother."

Some dude wearing a polyester sweater over his galabia tried to shove a sphinx carved of black stone into my hands. "Okay my friend, no problem, no charge."

Salah wandered ahead alone. Rosie rushed up to me and asked if she could walk with me. Oh no. I didn't know when she'd gotten the idea, but I was pretty sure that Rosie had decided that the two of us should hook up. All that stuff at breakfast about Octavia being crazy—she was clearly trying to turn me off of Octavia. I couldn't exactly say no, but I didn't want to be alone with Rosie either. "Yeah, sure. But I bet Mohammed would walk with you," I suggested, pointing out Octavia, who was skipping along with Mohammed, who was making sure no one pressed anything on her.

"Well, I kind of thought we could have a chat. On our own," Rosie added, looking at me significantly.

Crap.

She linked her arm though mine. The last thing I needed was Octavia thinking I liked Rosie. I pulled my arm away to point out Yo, who was stumbling by, swiping at something the rest of us couldn't see. The hustlers were all standing aside to let him pass, eyeing him up with his long, flailing limbs as if he were dangerous. "Check out Yo!" I said, laughing too loudly.

That was when the hustler took me aside and thrust a stone sphinx on me. I tried to give it back but he pressed it on me forcefully. "It bring you the heart of the one you love," he said with a wink. "You discover riddle, you win her heart, my friend." Now *that* was a sales pitch I could buy. I grabbed it and hugged it to my chest like the promise it was.

"You're not supposed to accept that," Rosie warned me. "Now you'll have to throw it on the ground."

I rebelled by doing what Octavia had suggested and said "*shookron*" instead.

"You're as bad as Octavia," Rosie told me, linking her arm though mine again.

I saw this as my chance to make myself clear. "Octavia's just the coolest, isn't she? Totally crazy. I've never met anyone like her," I continued. "She doesn't give a damn what anyone else thinks. She's just incredible and . . . I don't know, she's . . ."

"Hard work?" Rosie hazarded.

"Something special," I said firmly, pulling my arm away and tightly clutching the sphinx to my chest so she couldn't get her arm through mine again. And it was true, I didn't feel right about throwing a big carved stone sphinx on the ground. I had the riddle to consider. Astin had already thrown down a scarab, and that had caused a massive commotion among the vendors and got Mohammed into a push-and-shove situation with a bunch of hustlers. In the end, Astin handed the guy a large wad of cash just so he could get away. So much for Mohammed's great plan.

Octavia skipped up beside us. "You two make such a cute pair."

"We were having a *private* conversation," Rosie told her.

"No, we weren't," I argued. "Rosie was just telling me to smash the sphinx," I lied. "But I thought it looked too nice."

"Rosie!" Octavia chastized. "Darling, you're horrible. I love the sphinx! Don't you know that the sphinx is full of riddles and only if you solve them do all your dreams come true?"

Rosie rolled her eyes. "Octavia, you just made that up."

"It might be true," I insisted. "I mean, the guy who gave it to me said there was a riddle."

"Exactly. The ancient Egyptians were full of mystery and magic. Anyway, I'm proud of you for not following Mohammed's orders, Sam. Rosie, you shouldn't try and quell Sam's independent spirit. Did you see what Astin did to that poor man's beetle?"

"Scarab," Rosie corrected. "It's called a scarab."

"Yeah that *beetle* must have taken someone a lot of work to make," I agreed.

Then I made a few mental calculations.

1. Octavia admired my style and my independent spirit. Cool.

2. She thought Rosie and I made a cute couple. Terrible!

3. Solution: I needed to figure out that riddle to fulfill the prophecy.

. . .

By the time we reached the temple, I had also acquired an Arab headdress, a T-shirt with Tutankhamen across it, and a scarab like the one Astin had smashed.

Once we reached the temple, I put on my Knicks hat, carried the water by hand, wrapped the sphinx and scarab up in the Arab headdress, and swapped my shirt for the Tut T-shirt worn inside out. I looked like the worst kind of American tourist.

"Gee, you look swell," Octavia teased.

"Why, thank you, ma'am!" I tipped my cap.

The sun was beating down. Mohammed started his talk over all the other tour guides' voices. Astin was listening to his iPod with Salah—an earpiece each. Yo kept calling out, "Aaaah! Got cha! No prisoners!" to somebody or something in his visor. Eventually Mohammed asked to see what was going on. Yo gave him a brief rundown of the game, put the visor on his head, and that was all it took to hook Mohammed. He was at war with the tomb mummies.

Mr. Bell took over tour-guide duties. "We'll start with the majestic tomb of Rameses II's wife, Queen Nefertari. The greatest love story of ancient Egypt," he said with a sigh. Then he took the water bottle from his hat and took a drink.

The tombs were reached by a staircase roughly cut out of the rock.

Mohammed struggled down in the VR visor, crying out in Arabic, his arms flailing dangerously, his hands seemingly gripping virtual weapons as he battled his way through ancient Egypt. As hilarious as he looked, I was more interested in keeping an eye on Octavia. Aside from Rosie's one attempt to be alone with me, I was pretty certain Octavia was focusing on me. Maybe I'd been making too much of last night, I decided, and the incident with Salah really hadn't meant anything.

As we descended, Octavia took my hand. It was small and soft and warm in the cold, stale air of the tomb. We weren't permitted to take photographs, and although I noticed people trying to take sneak pictures with their cell phones, I wasn't even slightly tempted. It was the most eerily beautiful thing—and I didn't want to let go of Octavia's hand. No photograph could do this moment justice.

"It makes me feel quite reverent," Octavia whispered to me. "Like I should be kneeling or something."

I knew exactly what she meant.

On the way up the stairs, the heel of Octavia's shoe broke and I offered to carry her—along with my back-packs and cameras. It was the best feeling—holding her long, lean legs in my arms. I couldn't get enough of the feel of her skin. A guy at the entrance had gifted her with a horse-hair fan to shoo insects, which she used to playfully strike me as if I were a horse and she was my jockey.

Mr. Bell said, "Octavia, show some decorum," which was rich coming from a guy in a straw hat with a drink bottle sticking out the top.

When that didn't work, Mr. Bell implored me to, "Steady up, son!" which made Octavia giggle so hard she almost fell out of my arms.

"Oh no, I'm going to wet myself, dash for the loos, Sam, quickly," Octavia cried, swishing her horse-hair fan.

I'm not going to lie, I charged through the crowds—a compliant slave to her commands. I paid the five pounds demanded for her to use the filthy lavatories and waited for her in the sun. While I was waiting, I picked up a handful of sand and put it in my pocket. Then I took some shots of a collection of brightly colored plastic buckets piled outside the toilets. I had black-and-white film in, but the buckets had a translucent quality I figured would come out well.

Octavia was laughing when she emerged. "I swear you soooo don't want to *ever* know what went on in there."

"You're probably right," I agreed.

But she told all. "I had to squat, and, well, then afterward, I had to wash my feet with that hose thingamee they have. Only I misjudged the pressure somewhat and ended up drenching the poor little toilet woman. It was all very undignified."

I laughed, totally awed by her honesty. I mean, none of the girls I knew would want me to think of them as anything other than an object of beauty, but here was the most beautiful girl I'd ever met freely sharing her embarrassment.

It made her feel all the more real to me.

I hoisted her back into my arms, feeling genuinely connected to her—and not just her skin—for the first time.

We caught up with the rest of the group at Rameses II's tomb. Salah and Rosie were at opposite ends of the group, looking bored.

Mohammed was very much back in charge, Yo happily enjoying his virtual Egypt again. Mr. Bell looked pissed. "This tomb is that of maybe greatest pharaoh of Egypt. Rameses II," Mohammed explained. "As well as his wife, Nefertari, he had two hundred wives and concubines, ninety-six sons and over sixty daughters."

"So not the greatest romantic love after all," Octavia teased.

Mohammed smiled as he went on. "He fought many battles, smiting many enemies. For ninety-six years he live!" He paused so we could take all this in. "What is he most famous for, Mr. Bell, please?"

"Well, there's no doubt he led Egypt into a period of great prosperity," Mr. Bell said.

Mohammed grinned. "No, he is most revered for his great building program. The jewel in the crown of all his architecture was Abu Simbel. This proved to the world his glory! So why, Mr. Bell, did he build himself a hole in the ground to spend his afterlife?"

Bell took a gulp of water and was in the process of placing the bottle back in the crown of his hat. "Perhaps he was murdered. A lot of these chaps were, blood-thirsty lot don't you know. Poisonings were rife."

"Murdered at ninety-six?" Mohammed laughed dismissively. "No, he dug up and buried in large tomb in Abu Simbel. Quickly now, no more talk. The boat sails at noon."

Octavia giggled and insisted on riding on my back down the narrow wooden staircase to the tomb, crying, "Quickly, Sam, we sail at noon."

The tomb was just as Mohammed had tried to warn us, a hole in the ground. There were a few colorful hieroglyphs on the roof and walls but nothing majorly impressive.

"It definitely lacks the wow power of his wife's tomb," Carol chattered.

"Yeah, well, his wife was quite powerful in her own right," Ms. Doyle explained.

Mohammed shushed them. "Do you want to sleep on the banks of the Nile tonight?"

"Oh, darling, can we?" Octavia clapped, which made Mohammed smile.

We took a little train of open carts called *tuf-fufs* to the entrance. When we got there, the hustlers started chasing us for their "gifts," but they didn't recognize me. Instead of the guy in the white linen Ralph Lauren shirt, they saw a dopey Knicks fan in an inside out T-shirt carrying his girlfriend on his back. It was a proud moment.

Besides, Octavia and her broken shoe were getting all the attention. "No shoe? Why no shoe? This crazy! You American. You crazy people."

Next to me on the coach, she asked what was up with Salah. I shrugged. "He's moody like that," I lied, and I promise you, I didn't feel even slightly guilty about dissing my friend. "So Rosie told me that you're some kind of royalty. What's up with that?"

"You tell me, American boy," she said, giving me a shove. "What is up with that?"

"Nothing. You just don't *act* royal."

"How insulting. Anyway I don't need to *act* royal!" she teased, tipping my cap.

"Seriously though, tell me about it. I'm intrigued about stuff like that. We don't have lords or duchesses in America."

"Well, actually you might be disappointed. Being the daughter of a lord doesn't do as much for a girl as it used to. Especially when your father's an impoverished lord."

I was surprised by the sudden seriousness of her tone.

"Impoverished? You?" I squeezed her leg. "Those shoes you just broke must have cost more than the locals here earn in a year."

"A freebie from some stupid modeling shoot I did," she dismissed, sounding irritated. "Can we not talk about this, actually?"

"Sure. Sorry, I'm being nosey. It's an American thing and you're right, it's totally none of my business."

She stroked my head. "No, I'm sorry. I'm being horrible. I'm the biggest sticky beak, so I can hardly expect you not to ask about me. You can still call me M'lady if you wish." She giggled and that strange moment of tension between us was over.

I'd definitely got under her skin though and that made me feel unreasonably good. "Okay M'lady, you're on," I told her, grabbing her in a playful headlock, which worked well as an excuse to sneak an arm around her.

She took the Knicks hat off my head and hit me with it. "Americans are such dorks. And New Yorkers, well they're the biggest dorks of all."

And then she kissed me. It was only a light kiss. The sort an old aunt might give you, but it was a kiss and it was on the lips and in that moment, I closed my eyes and pretended it was a real kiss and forgot all about Salah. It lasted only one moment, but when that moment was over, I was resolved to do whatever it took to get a real kiss. She'd respected me for not throwing the sphinx down, and whatever had happened between us when I'd asked about her family had been real, and I knew that I could win that kiss. All I needed was more time.

CHAPTER 10

·•♥ OCTAVIA ♥•·

It's a dreadful thing that boys force girls to be so calculating.

Oh bugger, I'd just told Sam I was impoverished. Impoverished? Who talks like that? What an absolute tosser I am. And even though I got the bright idea to kiss him straight after I'd said it, to make him forget, I wasn't convinced my distraction had worked.

And what on earth had possessed me to open up to *him* of all people? I'd managed a lifetime of concealing the truth and then I go and blurt it to the best mate of the guy I'm trying to pull. Stupid, stupid, enormous-mouthed Octavia! I could just picture Sam blabbing to Salah and then Salah feeling all sorry for me and then . . . well, of course no boy wants to pull an object of pity. And then it occurred to me that it could even go further than ruining my Nile romance. What if Sam told

Salah and then Salah told Yo and Astin and they told Perdie and Artimis? It wouldn't take long before the whole school knew. I may as well have taken an ad out in *The Tatler*.

I wished I could have talked to Rosie about it but that would mean admitting I'd been lying all my life to her, too. Instead I decided to fish. "So, darling, do you think I had Salah seething with jealousy today, seeing me gallivanting around with Sam?" I asked her while I was showering off the sweat and desert sand.

"Oh yes, all that gallivanting is bound to make any boy seethe," Rosie agreed.

"I hope you weren't jealous darling? You know I'm not *after* Sam, right? He's just so much fun. I wish Salah was a bit more like Sam, actually."

Rosie didn't say anything, so I continued. "So, you really think a dark cloud of jealous despair descended upon Salah? Was he crying at any point do you think, Rosie?"

"Bawling his crybaby eyes out," Rosie assured me. "It was heartbreaking to watch. Really, rather pathetic. No one knew quite what to do."

I was enjoying bantering with Rosie. It was totally taking my mind off the Secret Impoverishment Thing. "So, do you think he'll get on his hands and knees and beg me to pull him?"

"I wouldn't really know about that, Octavia. I've never had a boy on his hands and knees begging for anything."

I turned the shower off. "Well, in that case, that is definitely something we shall remedy tout de suite. I noticed Sam gazing into your eyes at breakfast. I'm sure you could make him beg if you tried."

I toweled off and swept my clothes off the floor to make way for Rosie. "Shower's yours now," I told her, flopping on the bed beside hers. I looked up wistfully at the fabby Arabesque lantern hanging from the ceiling. It was a boat designed for love.

While Rosie showered, I threw myself into the task of dressing to slay. I'd only just finished emptying the contents of my suitcase on the bed when I looked out the window and saw that we were actually sailing down the Nile! I mean, of course one expects that sort of thing on a Nile cruise, but it was all just too exciting. I pulled up the wooden blind for a better view. There were a few feluccas sailing past. "Oh, Rosie, come and see this, we're actually sailing down the Nile, just like Cleopatra, only sans the golden barge contraption." But Rosie had the shower going and was humming away loudly.

I pressed my face against the window. It was all so timeless and glorious and romantic. Too perfect to waste. I absolutely completely had to make Salah love me.

"Rosie, you've got to hurry up," I begged, because I wanted to share the moment with her. Also, I was in a huge rush to get up to my Mark Antony.

But Rosie took forever and we arrived at an all but

empty restaurant. No one else (well, apart from the teachers) was there. One look at the diminished buffet suggested everyone had already grazed and run. The waiters were clearing away plates. I was so cross and frustrated at Rosie for spending so long in the shower and then taking forever to get dressed.

"Oh well, c'est la vie, I wasn't really hungry anyway. Shall we go and find the others?" I suggested, trying to hide my disappointment.

"But I'm famished," Rosie insisted belligerently.

I grumped over to the buffet, piled a bunch of salad leaves on a plate, and handed the nourishing cargo over to her. "Fine! Take this up with you then," I told her. "The green leaves match your skirt. Sam strikes me as the sort of boy to notice those details." Then before she could make a fuss, I shoved a bun in her mouth and strode out of the restaurant, up the stairs to the bar, and then outside to the lower deck.

Rosie could yell at me later. I had damage control to attend to.

"Hey!" Sam called from the other end, where he and Salah were stretched out on one of the white sofas under the canopy. He was adjusting the lens of one of his fancy cameras. I gave him a flirty wave and headed over. I could hear Rosie clunking up the stairs behind me.

Along the river's edge, women in black were spreading colorful rugs out on the mud brick walls. As I sat down, I pointed them out to the boys. "Aren't they picturesque, darlings?"

"You mean poor?" Salah replied as Rosie joined us.

The word made me go cold. "No, I mean pretty," I persisted. I couldn't bear for him to misunderstand me. What would he know about poor anyway? I looked nervously at Sam to try and work out if he'd blabbed anything.

"The colors of the rugs actually, they're just so vibrant and *rich*," I added pointedly.

"I agree," Sam said. He'd been fiddling with his Black-Berry but he put it aside and grabbed his camera again. "I'm a fan of the scene myself. A big fan of the donkeys especially. Check out that one over there," he said, taking a shot of a donkey on the bank. Then he showed me his camera screen and scrolled through some shots he'd taken earlier. I noticed there were loads of me, but before I could comment he stopped on a photograph of a donkey. "This little white one here especially caught my eye. How much do you think one of those would cost to ship back home, dude?" he asked Salah. "We could keep it at school."

Salah just smiled lazily.

"I think it's all amazingly beautiful," Rosie said as she speared a lettuce leaf with her fork and plonked herself inconveniently close to Salah. "I love the way the date palms and the green fields are all on one side and the golden desert and the mountains are on the other. The only thing is, it's sort of in total contrast to us." She gestured with her fork. "The luxury of this boat, I mean, all this food even!" she added, before jamming the leaf into her mouth.

Salah smiled again, and ran a hand through his hair, but said nothing. He looked so languid and fit. Although when he stretched and settled his hand back behind his neck, it was virtually touching Rosie. Mind you, boys have no sense of spatial reality. Still, Rosie could have shifted a bit—and shut up about poverty contrasts.

Not that it mattered because a moment later Salah's text alert sounded and he stood up and said, "I'm going to go check my e-mail."

"Good idea," Sam agreed as he gathered up his camera equipment and followed.

When I was certain they couldn't hear, I slipped over to Rosie's sofa. "They'd better bloody well be off to talk about *us* darling, or I shall have to do something drastic."

"Like what?" she asked.

"I haven't decided, but it's a dreadful thing that boys force us girls to be so calculating, that's all I can say."

"I don't think they do," she replied. "Force us to calculate, I mean. I don't think my brothers think too hard about things really. If they fancy a girl, they just make a move, you know, call her up or just make it obvious. I don't want to calculate."

"Well, I don't see how you expect to pull Sam if you don't brush up on your calculating skills."

"Maybe I don't *want* to pull Sam," she told me, looking me straight in they eye with a determination I'd never seen before.

CHAPTER 11

••• SALAH •••

*Sometimes when I'm with my friends and they talk about
girls and love, I have to wonder where their brains are.*

My mind was constantly on Rosie. Everything about her fascinated me. It was like everything I saw or experienced I wanted to see and experience through her eyes—and her music. It had been in my head since I'd first heard the piece she composed. I felt like her music really expressed how I felt about her. I wanted to talk to her about her music not as some sort of idle chat but because I wanted to find out what was behind it all. What was behind her mattered to me. But since the previous night I found myself tongue-tied around her.

Sam seemed to be doing better with Octavia in that they had hung out at the Valley of the Kings and Queens, but Octavia was still throwing herself at me. Sam and I had agreed an emergency girl-summit was required. So that afternoon, Sam texted the guys and we gathered with Astin and Yo in the computer room.

Yo and Astin were already on e-mail when we arrived.

"So, what's this problem with Octavia and Rosie?" Astin asked without looking up from the screen. "You dragged us away from our girls."

Sam and I admitted that we'd totally failed to figure out Octavia and Rosie.

"I told you, Salah, you should have filled in the Hottie Chart while you had the chance," Yo said. "Hey, do you think I can cut and paste the e-mail I'm sending to my mom and send it to my father as well? Do parents cross-check these things?"

"No," Astin assured him. "They barely talk. I always cut and paste."

"Yeah, so the Hottie Chart," Yo explained, spinning around and looking at me. "When it comes to scoring hot girls on school trips, it's all in the Hottie Chart. People who write stuff down make it happen."

As much as I loathed the whole thing, the truth was I was low on options.

So when Yo produced his Hottie Chart, I read it through. It had gone through several amendments as people had begun pairing off. I'm not proud of it even now, but under pressure from Sam, Astin, and Yo I gave in. "Okay, hand me the pen," I said, and then I gave a zero score to Octavia and all the other girls and put a ten plus next to Rosie's name.

"I hope you're genuinely committed to that score," Sam said when it was passed around. His voice had a weird tone to it even though he made it sound like he was joking around.

"What's your point?" I asked, but Astin ruffled my hair and sat me down for one of his dumb this-is-how-it-is talks. "Okay, Salah, so Rosie's your target. What are you going to do about it?"

"I have a plan," I lied.

Everyone laughed because I never plan my love life. It's one of those things that just arranges itself. Girls pursue you and you either respond or not. But actually, I *was* kind of formulating a plan. Nothing concrete, but I figured the Nubian show on the itinerary for that night might be a good time to make a move.

"Okay, here's your plan. We're all invited to watch *Death on the Nile* in Perdie and Artimis's room," Yo said. "Why don't you guys join us there around eleven? Maybe our lovin' will be infectious."

I swear to God I don't know how he gets away with saying stuff like that.

"Could," Sam agreed, "but unlike Mr. Hopeful here," he added, nudging me, "I've *actually* got a plan."

"What's that?" Astin asked.

"Remember all that loot I got away with at the Valley of the Kings? I was thinking of kind of taking Octavia aside and giving it to her. Mohammed helped me out at lunch with the Egyptian mythology surrounding the scarab, which is pretty cool. And then there's the sphinx thing. You know half lion, half man?"

"I know where you're coming from." Astin nodded sagely, rubbing his chin. "Seduction by mysticism."

"You think she's that sort of girl?" Yo asked as he put on his visor. Sometimes I actually think he looks weird without his VR gear on.

"Listen, all girls love the mystic stuff," Astin insisted. "But you need more than just some junky story and a couple of souvenirs. What did Mohammed give you?"

Sam pulled out some notes and scanned them. "Okay, so in a nutshell, the Sphinx is in Cairo and Octavia was right, the story goes that only if you solve the riddle of the Sphinx do you win the heart of the girl you love. Only I don't know the answer."

"So make it up, man," Astin told me. "Girls are like riddles. Who can figure them out?"

"Yeah, cool. Anyway, so the scarab symbolizes life and—"

"Let me jump in here," Astin interrupted. "You're not going to get anywhere with crap like that. I'm only helping because I'm your friend and I'm relying on you to do my physics homework for me when we get home.

But I promise you, Octavia's going to need a lot more than a beetle and a plaster sphinx."

"It's stone."

"Plaster, stone, whatever. As tools of seduction, they're just not happening."

"True. That girl is high maintenance," Yo agreed before he suddenly leapt up and swiped the air. "Damn, he got away."

We all nodded.

"So, this is what you do," Astin continued. "Punch it up. Make it sound like you're giving her special powers. Like, with the beetle, say it brings immortality. And as for the sphinx, say—"

"No, no, no," Yo interrupted, pulling off his visor. "The riddle. The riddle doesn't have anything to do with love. I worked out the riddle on level five. It's all about the progression from babyhood to becoming an old man. That's not going to romance anyone."

Astin pressed the send button on his e-mail. "You don't have to forget the riddle. You could work out a different riddle. Like, the one you love is closer than you think."

Sam threw a pencil at him.

Astin slapped the desk. "Believe me, the smulchier the better. You can never go too far with the gooey stuff."

"And I bet that Octavia chick has heard a lot of gooey stuff. You definitely need to top anything she's heard before," Yo added.

Sam was nodding and scribbling down Yo and Astin's sage advice.

"And make sure you mystify the whole experience too, dude," Astin said. "Give it the works—candles, cushions, the whole nine yards."

"Yeah, girls totally love effort. I think coming up with a rocking riddle would seal the deal," Yo insisted, slipping back to his virtual world.

"Yeah, but what can the riddle be?" Sam asked.

They all shrugged their shoulders.

I shook my head. Sometimes when I'm with my friends and they talk like that about girls and love, I have to wonder where their brains are. Astin was bobbing his head away to some song he'd downloaded while he'd been sending his e-mails and seemed disinterested in taking the discussion further. I looked out the portal and watched life on the Nile. There was a felucca of fisherman pulling in their catch and I wished I was sharing the sight with Rosie. Like the way we talked about the night sky and my history. See, that was the thing—Rosie got Egypt. Really got it, and being here again made Egypt feel that much more important to me than it had for a long time. Watching my friends, I felt weirdly detached from them and their view of the world. I stood up to go, but Sam stayed to get more info from Astin on his scene-setting theory.

. . .

Things eventually got going around ten that night when the DJ (also known as the front-desk guy) slid the disk effortlessly from an ancient Britney Spears number into the thumping drumbeats of Nubian music.

The lights dimmed, the circular dance floor lit up, and eight of our young Egyptian waiters—not a Nubian among them—wandered into the disco in makeshift costumes and bare feet. They were followed by two of the guys I'd seen cleaning the rooms, now belting away furiously on Egyptian drums.

The waiters formed a circle in the center of the room, held hands, and began to stomp in and out of the circle, raising their hands and clapping in beat to the drums while making a loud noise, which I think was supposed to sound like Nubian singing.

Octavia said something to Sam that I didn't catch, and the two of them slipped outside. The teachers were otherwise engaged, clapping in a vain attempt to keep time with the music. The dancers seemed to take encouragement from their clapping. They spread out and beckoned to the teachers to join them on the dance floor.

Carol didn't hesitate (of course) and swiftly pulled Nigel up to join her. He was wearing a cravat that evening, which Carol pulled off him, exposing an overabundance of gray chest hair. Mr. Bell and Ms. Doyle were cajoled by the waiters to dance. Soon the whole room was clapping and hooting as we watched our teachers clasp hands with the "Nubians." Some of the other guys crowded around the dance floor with girls, calling out, "Way to go!" and catcalling. Carol was loving the attention. Mohammed was the only adult there with the dignity to refuse the offer.

Yo and Astin saw this as their opportunity to start making out with their girls.

Eventually the teachers had enough. That's when the Nubians turned their attention to us.

I don't dance. I never have, and never plan to. But something shifted in me that night as the "Nubians" clustered around Rosie like a cult.

She looked like she was about to refuse, and suddenly, I don't know what came over me but I just knew I had to act. With Sam and Octavia out on the deck, this might be one of my few chances alone with Rosie. I jumped up, dragging her after me.

The dancers flanked each one of us, probably so we could learn the dance moves as much as to prevent us escaping. Rosie looked reluctant but joined in. I saw my chance, took her hand, and pulled her into me. But as incredible as it was to be holding her, I couldn't tell what her thoughts were. Had she forgiven me? What if I'd totally blown it, letting Octavia get away with that kiss? I racked my brain for anything that I should, or could, say.

Sam and Octavia returned as the dance was ending, but I tried not to let go of Rosie's hand.

"So, are we going to join the guys in Artimis and Perdie's room?" Sam asked.

"I might go up on the deck," I replied, "looking at Rosie. Look at the stars again."

"I'll join you," Octavia announced.

But I was saved by Sam. "Come on, man. Yo and Astin are expecting us. *Remember*?"

"That's right," I agreed. What the hell. Maybe a dark room would give me an opportunity to get close to Rosie.

Once we'd agreed on Sam's romantic plan that afternoon, he had gone alone to our room to set the scene for Octavia. Astin had offered to help him.

The film had already started when Rosie, Octavia, and I arrived at the girls' room. Inspector Poirot was looking out on the Nile in the garden of the Cataract Hotel in Aswan. Rosie sat at my feet, clutching her knees into her chest. She was soon as absorbed in the DVD as I was in the long strawberry-blond tangle of curls that was touching my knee. I was just about to reach out to touch her hair when Octavia stretched out on the bed and rested her head on my knee.

I swear to God it was like I was in some sort of Shakespearean farce. Only not a funny one. Maybe a tragedy? I wanted to ask Octavia to move away but I just didn't see how I could without drawing Rosie's attention. I might not be a player, but I know the cardinal rule: never show interest in the best friend of the girl you're after.

But the major reason I didn't want to disturb the moment was I'd finally gotten up the nerve to touch Rosie's hair, and I wasn't going to stop now for anything. I tried to dislodge Octavia by twitching my knee, but she only snuggled up closer. If anything, I'd managed to make things worse. My only chance was Sam. I kept willing him to return and save me. What kind of friend was he? In the meantime, I reached out my hand and began running it through the soft tendrils of Rosie's hair. She remained perfectly still as I ran my fingers along the back of her neck. I could feel the goose bumps rising in both of us. And then my hand got stuck in a tangle of Rosie's hair, and as I reached out with my other arm to free it, I caught Octavia's chin in the crook of my elbow. Perfect, now I was practically glued to both of them.

Just then the door opened, flooding the room with light from the corridor. Relief surged through me as Astin and Sam walked in.

I looked up at Sam and smiled with relief. For one crazy moment I thought he might see the funny side of my predicament. But I suddenly saw how it must look to him and realized that he wasn't going to save me at all. I was like a kid caught with both hands in the cookie jar.

I pushed both of the girls away before I realized my mistake. I practically scalped Rosie.

"Ouch!" she cried, turning around just in time to catch Octavia looking up at me with a sexy pout.

Just great!

Octavia suddenly grasped my other hand tightly to her chest.

"Octavia," I said, shaking her off realizing I needed to speak *for* Sam since he was either too stunned or too furious to speak for himself. "Sam's got this awesome surprise for you in his room."

"Yeah, it's awesome," agreed Astin. Nestling on the bed with Artimis, he began to kiss her, totally oblivious to everything.

"But we're watching the movie just now," Octavia explained, even though there was no way she could have seen the screen from her vantage point on my knee. "I'll come and see your room another time, darling." With that, she waved Sam away like a fan bearer she no longer required.

If I was the sort of guy who cried, that would have been my moment.

From the death glare on Rosie's face, it was clear that she knew I'd been cozy with Octavia. I knew then I was totally screwed on every front. "I'll have a look if you want, Sam," she offered.

"Don't bother," Sam replied, and turned on his heel.

I followed him out of the room but he didn't look back. He took the stairs two at a time. "Hey Sam, wait up," I called out.

He turned around and looked straight through me. "Salah, whatever it is, I don't want to hear it."

Wednesday, Day 3
Nefertiti sails to Edfu

Sunrise: 06:25 Sunset: 17:58
Wake up at leisure
08:00–09:00 Breakfast in the Nefertiti restaurant
10:00 Visit the Temple of Edfu in horse carriages
12:00 *Nefertiti* sails to Kom Ombo
13:30 BBQ on pool deck
17:00 Teatime on the pool deck
19:00 Visit the Temple of Kom Ombo on foot
20:30 Egyptian dinner in the Nefertiti restaurant
22:00 Galabia party in the Ankh bar
Overnight in Kom Ombo

CHAPTER 12

··· ROSIE ···

What makes American boys tick?

Bloody Sam! Why, darling? Why? Why are Americans so useless at *amore*? Why did he have to ruin everything last night? Just when Salah and I were finally connecting." That was the last thing Octavia had said to me the night before. It was also the first thing she said to me the next morning as we lay in bed, enjoying the luxury of our first lie-in since arriving in Egypt. Well, by lie-in, I mean 7:30 a.m.

I had been through these sorts of issues with Octavia and the boys I fancied since we'd first started pulling boys. But this was the first time the target boy had given an indication that he actually preferred *me* to my friend.

Normally I would feel quite resigned about Octavia trumping me in love, but this was different. I really, really liked Salah in a way I hadn't liked any other boy. In the past it had never been much of a sacrifice to let Octavia pull any boy she wanted. But now I could see I'd created a monster who just presumed she could have her pick of boys.

I couldn't stop thinking of how I'd felt as Salah touched my neck. A shiver of excitement went through me, followed closely by the realization that Octavia was clueless as to how I felt. To how Salah felt for that matter. And I had only my wimpish self to blame.

"Salah was definitely about to deliver full frontal lip action, Rosie, I could tell. He could not have been any clearer! He had reached down, you see . . . If only Sam hadn't . . . Agghhh!" She started flailing about on the bed and kicking her legs in the air. "I could strangle him!" Then she started making strangling gestures.

I lay there wondering how I could tell her that when Salah reached down, it was to stroke *my* hair, and then wondering if I even really wanted to. Discovering that a guy *she* fancied, actually fancied someone else—her best friend at that—might very well kill Octavia. No. I had to sort this out on my own. I had to be the strong one for once.

"I think we should snub them both," I told her firmly as a plan began to form in my brain. One thing growing up with brothers teaches you, is the power of ignoring boys.

"Are you mad?" she screeched.

"Well, they're clearly in this together," I insisted, even though I don't think Sam had a clue. As a composer, I'm quite used to making things up as I go along and I was *really* thinking on my feet that morning. "At least until we work out what we are doing. After all, Salah *did* chase after Sam, didn't he, when he could have stayed with you?"

"That's true," Octavia acknowledged. "I hadn't thought of that. You should have chased after Sam, Rosie. Maybe if you talk to Salah . . . ?"

"Maybe," I said.

With that, Octavia jumped out of her bed and came over and climbed in with me for a cuddle. "That's why you're my best friend, Rosie. You're the wisest, cleverest, most darling creature in the world."

And at that moment as the plan took shape in my head, I had to agree with her.

. . .

Artimis and Perdie were sitting alone when we arrived at breakfast, so we joined them. Perdie was braiding her hair as usual. Artimis grabbed us and said, "Perdie went to second base with Yo last night. I went to third with Astin."

Yuck!

"Cool," I said. I looked at Octavia and asked her if she wanted me to get her breakfast. Turning to look at the buffet, she spotted Sam and Salah filling their plates and nodded. "Thank you, darling."

Right, Rosie, this is it, I thought. Confrontation. You must speak to Salah and sort out this whole mess, I told myself as I hovered near the buffet. I tried to listen to what they were saying, but all I heard was silence.

Something wasn't right. I grabbed a few pastries and returned to the table where the girls were all laughing.

"Oh, darling, is that all you got me? I'm famished!" Octavia cried, her lower lip curled like a little child's. But as her eyes darted in the boys' direction, I knew that what she was really saying was, "What are the boys talking about?"

Before I could reply, Sam stormed past our table and left the restaurant, virtually knocking over a waiter carrying a large tray of cheeses.

"Just a minute, I have to go to the loo," I told Octavia, and raced out after Sam. The truth is, I had no idea what I was going to say to Sam, but I needed some answers if there was any chance of sorting out the four-way love square Octavia, Sam, Salah, and I had fallen into.

"Great idea, darling. You go after Sam and give Salah a chance to speak to me on his own," Octavia said. She really had no idea.

"Hey Sam, wait," I called as he flew down the stairs to reception. He didn't seem to hear me. I couldn't tell if he was intentionally snubbing me or genuinely hadn't heard.

After chasing him down the long, narrow corridor, I finally caught up with him as he was opening the door to his cabin. "Rosie? What's up?" he asked as he turned to face me. He seemed genuinely surprised that I had been following him.

I was a bit out of breath, and now that I was face-to-face with him I couldn't for the life of me think of a thing to say. I just knew I had to say something. "Can I come in for a moment?" I asked.

"Uh, maybe that's not such a good idea. Pretty gross in here. You know, Salah's socks." He pinched his nose.

"Oh, okay," I agreed. "Look, do you have any idea what went on last . . ." I stopped short as I caught a glimpse of the interior of their room through the crack. I mean, it was just like all the other cabins except for one thing. There were hundreds—I'm not exaggerating—hundreds of small, brightly colored glass candleholders over every surface and large Egyptian-fabric-covered cushions thrown across the floor.

I tried to get a better look but Sam pulled the door closed. "Sam? What was that?" I demanded.

"What was what?"

"All those candles and cushions," I said. After years of being Octavia's best friend I've learned a thing or two about dogged persistence. "Look Sam, I'm not an idiot. You know what I saw in there. It looked like a . . . like a . . . well, some sort of harem affair. What are you and Salah up to?" There were lots and lots of thoughts running riot in my head.

Sam opened the door. "It has nothing to do with Salah."

"Then what?"

"Wasted love. An exercise in futility by Sam, now showing on a Nile cruise near you. It was a stupid idea," he explained.

"I don't understand. This was for Octavia?"

"I was going to give her the scarab and the sphinx I got at the Valley of the Kings and Queens yesterday. Only then, Astin said I needed to set the scene. Hence the candles and cushions. Dumb, huh? I don't know what I was thinking. I mean, why would a girl like Octavia . . ." His sentence trailed off again, and he ran his hand across his face as if trying to wake himself up from a dream. "I must have been crazy to think I had a chance."

He seemed so very young and vulnerable at that moment, and I felt so uncharacteristically strong and un-me. And I liked it. I took his hand, pulled him into the room, and put my hands on his shoulders. I was about his height in heels, thank goodness, or I would have felt like a dwarf talking to a giant. "Sam," I said authoritatively.

"Rosie," he said, his mouth turning up in a small smile.

"You love crazy, right?"

He grinned and nodded.

"Well, as the best friend of the craziest girl in the world, trust me, I know a thing or two about crazy. Crazy is a lot of hard work." Then I pushed him and he fell back on the bed. "But mostly it's worth it. That is, if you're up for the challenge?"

"Oh, I'm up for it!" he insisted.

"If you want a chance with a girl like Octavia, you need to think carefully about two things. First, *every* boy wants to pull a girl like Octavia. So, Octavia expects to be chased and pursued and obsessed over. That's all she knows. Next, think about why she's *so* into Salah, when as far as I can see, he's practically ignored her the entire time."

"So, what you're saying is, I should ignore her?"

"No. I'm just saying that you should think about those two things. I haven't told you what you have to *do* yet."

He was gripped and even I was feeling caught up in the plan. "So, with every guy on the planet falling over themselves for Octavia, how many of them do you think take the time to really get to know her?" I said.

Sam shrugged, but I could see his mind was turning this idea over.

"Exactly. They're too busy fighting off their competition to get inside her head and heart, too frantically obsessed to want to find out about the real Octavia."

"So, I should . . ."

"Stop thinking about your competition, because you know what? You haven't got any. So take the time, Sam. Take the time."

"Take the time," he repeated.

CHAPTER 13

··· SAM ···

The Feast of the Beautiful Meeting

So, we take the horse and carriage. In Egypt this is called caleche," Mohammed explained once we were all gathered in reception.

"Each caleche takes four peoples and will take you through the town and on to Edfu Temple. This is the second largest and most perfect preserved temple in all of Egypt. We do security check, then after we do a small blah, blah outside, not long because I know you English, you go a little crazy in the heat. Americans, you already crazy peoples." Mohammed laughed and put on his Indiana Jones hat.

"Then inside the temple, we study magnificence of the ancient Egyptians. But this temple has a roof. It's very cold, so take a jacket. After two hours, we return and sail to Kom Ombo. Okay, any questions?"

No one said anything.

"So, four to a carriage."

Rosie and Octavia were ahead of us. Salah and I were at the back because all our boys had paired up with their girls. School trips are meant to be about hot girls in foreign countries, but somehow, Salah and I were turning into the Odd Couple. The only two guys who *hadn't* paired off. But after Rosie's talk that morning, I was more fired up than ever to make a move on Octavia. And that meant that Salah and I needed to join their caleche.

Salah wasn't fired up though, so I had to literally grab him by his suit lapel and drag him down the red-carpeted gangplank and out to the carriages. Each carriage had a brightly colored canopy, so I had to check inside to see who was sitting there.

Eventually I found Octavia and Rosie in one of the front carriages. Unfortunately, Astin and Artimis were already seated opposite them on a small bench seat behind the driver.

"Hey dude, would you mind?" I asked, and Astin wasn't the sort of guy you needed to ask twice. He and Artimis jumped out.

"Darling," Octavia said, only she wasn't talking to me. I pushed Salah up into the carriage and I'd barely climbed in behind him when the driver flicked his whip and we were off. Rosie gave me a small smile of encouragement.

We passed through a dusty, smelly, fly-ridden town built of mud brick and cement. I took some shots of plastic-sandaled feet walking along the dirt streets. Vendors selling vegetables, women carrying bags with boxes on their heads, and of course the standard donkey shots.

"So, Octavia and I were wondering if photography was your thing, Sam?" Rosie asked.

"We were?" Octavia exclaimed, clearly surprised.

"Yeah," I said, directing my answer to Octavia. "I'd like to have an exhibition of some of the shots I've taken here. I'm just not sure of my theme yet. Sometimes I think everything in Egypt is about color and then sometimes I think I should go for black and white or maybe sepia tones. It's something about the ancient feel of the place, the timelessness of it all and then suddenly you see giant transformers taking electricity from the dam in Aswan up to Cairo. It's the juxtaposition, know what I mean?"

Octavia nodded vaguely. "Arty sort of stuff, you mean?" adding, "I prefer sunbathing to photography." And then I was stumped for words about photography probably for the first time in my life. Salah ignored us both and turned to the driver to ask him something in Arabic.

At Edfu we had to walk through a large parking lot filled with buses and wait in the heat while Mohammed dealt with the security. Policemen wielding AK-47s were out in force. Some of them looked pretty trigger-happy, too—like they'd been manning their post for years and were getting pissed at still never having had the opportunity to open fire.

There was a long road of vendors selling galabias, belly-dance outfits, and other tourist junk, but we weren't hassled too badly. Eventually we were asked to put our backpacks through the metal detectors and we walked through into the temple complex.

Mohammed called out, "Nefertiti, follow me."

Without warning, Carol blew a whistle. Everyone around us panicked. Instantly the twitchy police were all over Carol like angry wasps. Every gun in the place was aimed at her head.

Instead of falling to the ground like a normal person, Carol started crying, "Police brutality!"

I guess Nigel saw his chance to step in and be the man of the moment, which was pretty laughable. "Look here, chaps. You're terrifying this poor lady," he squeaked. In spite of his attempt, a scuffle broke out and both Carol and Nigel were soon cuffed and led out of the complex at gunpoint by more than a dozen overly excited cops.

None of us knew what to do. Only Mohammed seemed satisfied with this turn of events. Mr. Bell and Ms. Doyle looked less sure. "I think that was a little extreme,"

Doyle muttered almost to herself. She didn't seem bothered enough to do anything about the situation any more than Mr. Bell did—though he offered her a drink from the bottle in his hat.

"It's okay," Salah assured the group. "They probably haven't been arrested, just asked to leave. They don't want troublemakers at the temples. Any nonsense, and visitors are automatically ejected."

Mohammed gathered us all together and we headed toward the entrance of the temple. The wall was covered with an amazing carving of a battle scene, and was about a hundred and fifty feet high. I took some random shots as I walked along. Feet, backpacks, tourists' faces, hieroglyphics, police, guns, and Octavia.

Mohammed had just started his talk when Salah headed off alone into the complex. Octavia followed him and Rosie gave me a look that made it clear I should follow Octavia.

I soon found Salah in the courtyard by a statue of Horus, the falcon-headed god. He didn't notice me, so once I'd established that Octavia wasn't with him, I slipped out and continued my search for her through the incredible maze of courtyards and chambers in the complex.

I eventually found Octavia in a chapel by herself, leaning against a pillar. She looked like an Egyptian goddess with her black hair streaming down her back.

She was dressed in a long, flowing white dress. I took a shot of her looking up at the sunlight that filtered in from the gap between the walls and the roof. She seemed so much a part of the fabric of the building that I was startled when she finally looked at me.

"Oh, it's you. I was looking for Salah. Have you seen him, darling?" she asked quietly.

"No," I lied, my heart sinking a little. How could she *still* want Salah?

She didn't move but she didn't look at me again either. Eventually she said, "I wanted him to find me in here," she explained. "This is where Hathor would come to spend a fortnight with her husband Horus every year. There were the maddest ceremonies associated with it. It was called the Feast of the Beautiful Meeting. I feel like it's my story. Now the only meetings going on are up there," she mused, pointing at the ceiling, which was crammed with pigeon nests. A pigeon flew in and darted straight back out.

"I wanted him to find me here," she repeated quickly. "I wanted a beautiful meeting," she concluded, still fixing her eyes on the ceiling.

"I found you," I said.

She smiled and moved away from the pillar. "Do you think he'll find me here?"

"He's probably on his way," I told her, because I was afraid that if I said anything else, she might leave and I would never have time alone with her again. Rosie's advice about getting to know the real Octavia was echoing in my head.

A crowd of Japanese tourists entered a few moments later and I took Octavia's hand and led her through the crowd and over to a narrow staircase, which seemed to lead up to somewhere. Octavia sat on one of the cold steps and hugged her knees. I was used to the wild extravert, but this subdued and vulnerable Octavia was intriguing. I needed to find out more about this girl.

I sat beside her, my own leg touching hers in the tightness of the stairwell. We sat silently as group after group and guide came in and did their thing. But we didn't say a word.

Finally our group arrived. Salah wasn't with them. Mohammed began his spiel about the Beautiful Meeting. "It was here, after the priests had dressed the statue of Horus and fed him and given him some entertainment, they took his statue up those stairs for the sex union with Hathor."

"It's always sex, sex, sex with you, Mohammed!" Octavia exclaimed to the delighted surprise of everyone as she suddenly jumped up from next to me, revealing herself to the group. I wanted to grab her, to hold on to the Octavia she'd just revealed to me. Not the wild Octavia she seemed to think she needed to be.

Mohammed blushed and fumbled with his hat in

embarrassment. "Okay, we are off!" he announced, and we were rushed off back to the waiting caleches.

"I wonder what could have happened to Salah," Octavia asked our group.

"Oh, he went back to the boat with Carol and Nigel," Rosie replied.

"Typical," Octavia said, rolling her eyes at me.

I looked up at Rosie and she winked.

CHAPTER 14

❖❖❖ OCTAVIA ❖❖❖

No wonder it's always down to the girls to do the pulling.

We were all gathered on the pool deck, lazily sipping on drinks and eating sweets and not really saying anything much. It was nice just enjoying the cool breeze and watching life on the Nile as we passed by.

Salah was wearing a cool white double-cuffed shirt, unbuttoned, which revealed his lovely brown tummy, which was positively rippling with muscles. He was maddeningly fit and *not* focusing on me. But for the first time, I really didn't care.

I mean, obviously it was mortifying that everyone—apart from Rosie—seemed to have paired up while I remained resolutely unpulled. Thank God there was no one from *Tatler* there to witness my loveless state. I would be laughed out of my mad little world.

I was so worried that Sam would say something about how I'd waited for Salah in the chamber of the Beautiful Meeting that I clung to them both at lunch. Afterward, I was desperate for the loo but I couldn't afford to leave my post. I couldn't risk Sam saying something that would make me appear desperately lovesick for Salah. Which I so wasn't. Anymore.

In fact, I was beginning to wish I'd never fancied Salah in the first place. Why had he kissed me when he rescued me from the Elderly Cruisers? Why had he let me put my head on his lap during the movie? On the other hand, Rosie would never have the confidence to pull Sam and have a lovely holiday romance if I didn't show her the way with Salah. And if anyone deserved a lovely holiday romance, it was Rosie. It was frustrating beyond belief.

I liked Sam. He was definitely good enough for Rosie. He'd been adorable to me all day. I'd told Rosie how kind he'd been that morning, so she wouldn't get jealous and think I was moving in on her boy, because I absolutely didn't see him in that way. No, Sam was a mate and nothing more. I loved that he was so much fun to hang out with. That afternoon Sam had gone swimming, and held me on his shoulders so I could dive off. We were just mucking about, but then I'd noticed Rosie watching us from the shade and I pulled myself out of the pool. I didn't want her getting the wrong idea about my feelings for Sam.

We pulled our clothes back on after we dried off so we could sit on the sofas and drink tea, but Sam's shiny black hair was still mussed up, which made him look quite rugged. I don't normally go for the rugged type, but for a split second I thought, I definitely could. Not that I'd ever steal a boy from Rosie. I'm so not that sort of girl. The thought hadn't crossed my mind.

Well, barely at all.

· · ·

The first plastic-wrapped bundle came hurtling through a gap in the canopy around five, followed by another and then another. They kept coming at us like missiles. Some fell in the pool, some hit us on the head, some just kerplopped at our feet. We could hear yelling from the Nile and everyone looked over the side of the boat to see what was going on.

A few dozen feluccas, manned by four to six men in turbans, had tethered themselves around the *Nefertiti* and were throwing galabias up for us. It was like *Pirates of the Caribbean*, only the pirates were frocked up in man dresses. Carol tore a wrapper off and held up a purple galabia with gold-painted markings and a ghoulish picture of Cleopatra in the middle. She wasted no time in wriggling her ample figure into it, her bosom contorting the face of Cleopatra into a big-headed blob. Carol was happy though. Old people are easily pleased. She started doing belly-dancing maneuvers to impress

Nigel. It was disturbing yet I couldn't look away. Sort of like a car wreck.

Mohammed called out, "If you want to buy, you put money in the plastic bag of another you don't want and throw back. The men, they share the money." Then he walked off into the bar.

All the guys were pulling off their shirts and trying on the long, dresslike galabias. Sam had already been through three by the time I tried on my first. He tried on a purple one like Carol's and shimmied up to her in it, shaking his shoulders like her, only he couldn't make his belly wobble in the same way. Carol went crimson. One of the crew was videoing the scene. It was definitely memorable, so I took a snap on my phone. When I checked the image, I saw I'd focused on Sam. Purely coincidence, I'm sure. Besides, Rosie might like it.

"Try this one, Nigel. It's your color," Carol insisted, holding out a brown galabia.

"I don't think so, Carol," he replied firmly, looking even stiffer than he usually does. His lips were all pursed.

"Look, even Liz and Brian are at it." She pointed over to Mr. Bell and Ms. Doyle, who were frolicking about like teenagers. It was quite literally a sight for sore eyes.

"Well, each to his own," Nigel insisted gruffly, smoothing down the lapels of his polyester safari jacket.

That's when Carol went bonkers and started grappling with the buttons on Nigel's shirt. I'd never seen anyone quite so overcome with lust—at least, that's what I assumed it was. Nigel put up quite a struggle, but Sam came to Carol's aid and held him down so she could strip him of any dignity he may have ever deluded himself he had.

The whole scene was chaos. The felucca men calling out, the galabias flying on and off the boat. I felt like the only grown-up on deck. Eventually even Nigel was happily throwing back an unwanted galabia with his payment for the one he had been squeezed into.

I looked over and saw Salah sitting on a sofa, quietly pretending to read a book. He was really looking at the other side of the deck, where Rosie was working on a music score. She really was mad, not joining in with everyone. No wonder she hadn't managed to pull Sam yet.

She couldn't have found a better opportunity to pull him if we'd planned this moment for a month. He was there for the taking. No shirt, high spirited, and being very, very affectionate. He placed his arm around me to support himself while we cracked up over the sight of all the teachers doing their conga line.

I didn't want to give Rosie the wrong idea about Sam and me, so I moved away, suggesting, "Sam, why don't you choose a costume for Rosie?"

"What's that?" he asked.

"Rosie," I repeated. No wonder it's always down to

the girls to do the pulling. "Look at her," I said, pointing over. "She's deep in composition mode, which is what makes her so exotic and interesting, don't you think?"

"I guess." He shrugged and made a face as if he wasn't completely besotted with her. Boys!

"Come on, she'll love it," I assured him, giving him a knowing nudge.

"Fine," he agreed disinterestedly as he grabbed a pink galabia from the deck and handed it to me. I was about to tell him to take it over to Rosie, but she suddenly stood up and cried out, "Oh look!" We all looked to where she was pointing, up the Nile.

Ahead of us there was an ancient ruin. More piles of pillars and rubble than a temple, but it was cool because it was the first impressive evidence of Ancient Egypt we'd actually seen from the river.

"Hey Mohammed, get out here," Astin called into the bar. "There's a ruin thing coming up. Check it out."

Like Mohammed hadn't seen enough ruins to last a lifetime.

"I think its Kom Ombo," Rosie said.

Salah went over to her, stood by her side, and whispered something in her ear, which was tremendously annoying and blatantly meant to make me jealous. But what about poor Sam!

We eventually docked at Kom Ombo as the sun was setting. By seven, the gangplank and red carpet were laid out and we all set off on foot to explore the town. All, except for Rosie. I tried pleading.

"Are you sure?" I asked.

"Totally, I need to get this piece down while it's still in my head. I'll catch up," she insisted.

I really am in awe of Rosie and her talent. I felt like such an airhead as I skipped down the gangplank and along a small dirt pathway lined with bustling cafes. The sun was nearly down and the aroma of coffee and the sweet scent of pipe smoke wafted into the air. I recognized a couple of chaps who'd been chucking galabias up at us earlier, but they were all solemn and dignified now.

I could see Sam's head, way up at the front of the straggling group, so I sidled up and put my hands over his eyes. I wasn't flirting or anything, it was just that Sam had been such a sweetie earlier that day at Edfu and I felt really close—*Oh my God!* I thought. *I so should not be having thoughts of closeness to Sam.* A horrible feeling of guilt descended on me, but I still let him pull me into him.

I nestled under his arm and we walked along. It felt nice hanging out with a guy as *friends*. Yes, I realized, that's all these feelings were. I'd never had a boy as a friend before. Well, not as a close friend that I could share the deepest and darkest with. Was that why I'd told Sam the truth about how poor my family was? I felt an incredible sense of relief at having shared the truth with someone. Even if he hadn't really understood. I'd never really had boys as friends. At some point I usually find they want a lot more.

"Now for the blah, blah, blah," Mohammed announced, clapping his hands to get our attention.

Sam still had his arm around me. I looked around for Salah because, well, there we were, standing on the dark steps of a temple, illuminated by floodlights: if this wasn't Salah's perfect chance to pull me, I don't know what was. And that's when it occurred to me that perhaps Salah was inside, waiting for me the way I'd waited for him at Edfu. That was exactly what I'd wanted that morning but not anymore . . . I was enjoying being snug under Sam's arm.

". . . known also as the Temple of the Crocodile because crocodiles used to sun themselves on the steps you stand on now. Watch your ankles, please!"

"Also known as the Temple of the Falcon, I think you'll find," Ms. Doyle added.

Mohammed ignored her. "The temple, which dates back to the Ptolemy's, has been inhabited by Coptic Christians and later by local villagers, who used the stones to build themselves houses. Inside there is still many interesting things we can accept. For example, surgical instruments just as they use in hospitals in London and New York to this very day."

"Perhaps that's pushing it a bit," muttered Nigel to appreciative guffaws from his fellow teachers.

"Speaking of pushing, we push on," Mohammed said grimly.

"Darling, aren't you getting a bit worried about Rosie?" I asked Sam, but really I was sort of hoping he wasn't.

"Who?"

I punched him in the arm. "Behave," I said, secretly pleased with his answer. Talk about conflicted!

"I am behaving," he replied, tickling me.

It was as I struggled with him that I felt an odd stirring of excitement. The worst part was, I didn't pull away when I had the chance. I honestly meant to. I thought about it. But I didn't. In fact, I did the opposite, and as I was pulling his hand away, I entwined my fingers in his. Then I let him take me by the hand and lead me to a small antechamber where the floodlights couldn't reach us. I let him take my face in his hands and I let him kiss me.

I keep saying "I let him," but actually, I've never in my life let a boy do anything I didn't want him to. I *wanted* Sam to kiss me. Looking back, I think I'd wanted him to kiss me since that morning at Edfu when he'd found me alone in the chamber. His kisses were gentle and delicious. I wish I could lie, but the truth is, I didn't think of Rosie once.

The guilt didn't hit me until we were approaching the boat and I saw Rosie and Salah sitting together on the deck. Rosie's head was bent over her composition and Salah was looking at her while pouring water. And then I had the most evil thought: it would be great if they got together. I was ashamed as soon as the thought occurred to me. I pulled my hand from Sam's as if it were a hot coal.

Sam looked bewildered, adorable, and upset.

"Darlings, there you are," I said. "You should have come with us. It was wonderful, wasn't it, Sam?" I asked, red-faced with guilt.

Rosie and Salah were both looking at me like I was mad.

I turned to Sam but he was storming off.

And it was then that it hit me hard, the full enormity of what I'd done and how many people's lives I had complicated. Had I been chasing the wrong boy all along?

"I think you should go after him, Octavia," Salah said. And so I ran off, confused and ashamed.

CHAPTER 15

··· SALAH ···

Even our best plans can lead to our own destruction.

I'm a big believer in fate, kismet, you know, the whole "God's will, not my will" thing. The point is, accepting your fate makes everything more relaxing. I watch people running around trying to bend the world to their own will and getting bent out of shape in the process. If you just kick back and let fate carry you along, it's a hell of a lot more peaceful. Well, that's how it had worked up until meeting Rosie. And now, I was fed up waiting for fate to make her mine.

Sam's always saying that life is what you make of it. So even though it went against all my principles and my belief in Allah's will, I'd decided it was time to take fate into my own hands. I was going to go after Rosie with everything I had.

I'd walked in on Sam and Octavia at Kom Ombo the previous night. Sam had finally managed to get her alone, and it looked like he was making progress. But there I was, wandering around alone while the girl I couldn't get out of my head was all alone back on the boat. I looked up at the stars and remembered the night we'd looked up at the stars and talked about Egypt.

Sam and Octavia had no idea I'd seen them. I'd run as fast as I could back to the boat, where Rosie was still working on her composition. She had her back to me and as I approached, I could hear her humming, "Dum, diddlie, dum, dum dee."

So, like the suave, sophisticated guy I am, I said, "Hey, is that your song?"

She turned to me. "It's not a song. It's a movement." Then she turned around again and left me standing there like an idiot.

Eventually I sat down across from her and picked up the composition sheets she was scrawling on. "Wow, that looks hard," I said. Hard? Had I just said *hard*? How old was I? Two?

She snatched the page back from me, shuffled the sheets into a pile, and put them in a folder. "Oh yes, very, very hard."

"Cool. I mean, good." I wanted to smack my head on the table. And that's exactly what I did. I leaned over and banged my head on the table several times.

Rosie said nothing. What could she say?

I stopped after a while. It hurt a little.

We sat in silence.

"So, music," I said, struggling to get a conversation off the ground. (And failing miserably.) "That's not something I know a lot about."

"Oh?" she replied.

"Funny thing is, Egyptian music has more notes."

She leaned forward and looked at me curiously. "More notes?"

"I think they're called quarter chords or half-half notes or something. That's why Arabic music sounds . . ." I groped for words like a drowning man. Help! What was the word I was looking for?

"Exotic? Complicated? I love it. I love the complexity. Do you mean quartertones?"

My face lit up. "Do I? Yeah, that's it, quarternotes."

"Quartertones," she corrected.

"Quartertones," I repeated. "Yeah, that's it." I tapped the table with my fingers and cleared my throat. Could I be any more stupid? Why had I decided to discuss music—a subject I knew nothing about—with a musical genius? I should have stuck with astronomy. The silence became more and more awkward, so I told her I was thirsty just to fill it. Then I poured myself a glass of water from a pitcher on the table. Not wanting to appear rude, I offered her some.

"Thanks," she replied.

Suddenly I realized there was only one glass. It must have been *her* water pitcher and *her* glass. I pushed the glass back toward her and poured some more water into it to show her I really meant it.

"No, honestly, you may as well have it," she told me. "I'm fine."

Great. Of course I knew what she was really saying. *"You may as well have my water now that you've helped yourself, you greedy self-centered American."*

I was dying. I was a dead man sitting and while I was sitting, thinking about my dead status, I looked at Rosie and continued to pour the water over the rim of her glass and into my lap. That was when it blurted out of me. "You don't like me, do you?"

She looked me straight in the eye with those big golden eyes of hers and replied, "What?"

I kept pouring the water down my pants.

And then Octavia and Sam turned up. And a whole new mess began.

<u>Thursday, Day 4</u>
Nefertiti sails to Aswan

Sunrise: 06:24 Sunset: 17:57
08:00 Wake-up call
08:00–09:00 Breakfast in the Nefertiti restaurant

09:30 Visit the Temple of Philae, the High Dam &
the unfinished Obelisk by bus
13:00 Lunch in the Nefertiti restaurant
15:00 Felucca trip around Elephantine Island
19:30 Dinner in the Nefertiti restaurant
Overnight in Aswan

CHAPTER 16

••• ROSIE •••

Sometimes revenge can taste annoyingly sweet.

Darling, we have to talk," Octavia announced the next morning as we were getting dressed for another hot bus journey. This time to Philae.

I really didn't want to talk. I had barely slept after the conversation with Salah the night before. I'd just ruined my life and I didn't care about anything or anyone else. I mean, Salah had made an effort to come and chat with me. In other words, it was my big break, my chance to show what a wonderful, interesting, charming, funny girl I could be. But then when he'd approached me to talk about music (which he clearly knew nothing about, bless him), I'd made him feel like a fool. I hated myself. I couldn't have been colder if I'd tried. "Octavia, I'm not really up for a chat right now. Let's just grab our water and get upstairs. We're late."

"Okay," she agreed hesitantly. "But honestly, I've done the most evil thing. I've behaved worse than that really, really horrible goddess that did that really mean thing to her son."

"Octavia, I can't."

"What I'm trying to say is, I know I told you Sam likes you and I know I said I liked Salah, but well, the thing is—" Only she didn't get to give me her confession because there was a knocking on the door. Octavia opened it and in walked Salah.

"Did we invite you into our room?" I asked, trying to sound teasing but probably sounding more like a prize cow.

"I won't stay . . . ," he began. Yes, I had definitely sounded like a prize cow.

"I brought you this. I mean, I wanted to give it to you earlier but then I poured water over everything and . . . just take it," he said, holding out a package. "I hope you like it. You can throw it out."

"How promising," Octavia said after he left. "Rosie, whatever did you say to make him feel so awkward? I'm starting to think I'm *not* the most evil girl in all the world, after all."

"You're not. I just can't seem to stop being horrible to him and . . ."

"That's what I always do when I fancy a boy. Torture

him. Oh my God!" she cried, stuffing her fist into her mouth as the penny finally dropped. "You fancy Salah, don't you!"

I went bright red.

"Oh Rosie, why didn't you say anything? Don't you see this is perfect!"

I stared at the package in front of me in disbelief, until finally Octavia announced, "Well, if you're not going to open his present, I will!"

"No!" I said as the tears banked up behind my eyes. "I'll open it," I told her, and as the ribbon gave way a pile of old sheet music fluttered to the floor.

I gathered up the pages and leafed through them.

"Wow!" Octavia said. "He must be pretty keen to buy you such a perfect gift. And where and how did he manage to get hold of them?"

I ran my hand over the scores, the music already seeping into my fingers, suffusing my brain.

Octavia babbled away as the music played on in my head. "He must have used family connections. I think you and he make a perfect couple. I don't feel the least bit evil about stealing Sam. I really don't know why you pretended to like Sam all that time . . ."

Eventually I looked at her and said, "Salah bought me these."

"Well, of course he did," Octavia said, rolling her eyes with a laugh.

"There's a card too," she added, chucking an envelope at me. "He must really like you!"

I went red, and then even redder, as I scanned the letter.

Rosie,

Here's some Bach I had a guy get from town. My dad tells me that Bach's the composer's composer, so I hope you like it.

Something tells me you're a better composer than I am a poet, but I'm hoping if I show you my offering, you might consider sharing yours sometime?

P.S. Feel free to laugh. Sam did.

For Rosie
A disk of sun with light descending
Splits the mind, a shrine unfolds
As light attends to touch the temple
Through the sense of notes unending.

Friday, Day 5
Nefertiti docked at Aswan

Sunrise: 06:24 Sunset: 17:57
Wake up at leisure

Free day of escorted shopping in Aswan
13:30 Lunch in Nefertiti restaurant
18:00 Video demonstration of your cruise in the
        Ankh bar
20:00 BBQ dinner on pool deck
Evening at leisure
Overnight in Aswan

CHAPTER 17

♥♥♥ SAM ♥♥♥

The riddle of the sphinx:
Q: What creature has two hearts?

I finally gave Octavia my riddle scrawled on a piece of repro parchment we had in our rooms for stationery. I'd struggled long and hard with my riddle. I wanted her to know how I felt without sounding lame. I hadn't asked for any help from Salah, which, as I passed over the envelope, I suddenly decided was a big mistake.

Octavia read it and gave me a significant look. I guess I thought she was about to laugh. "It's just a joke," I told her, grinning stupidly and wondering why on Earth I hadn't run my riddle by Salah or Rosie first—or even Mohammed, for that matter.

I turned to the comfort of my camera. I was photographing the mast from which the large white sail billowed, but I was really spying on Octavia out of the corner of my eye. She trailed her hand over the railing. "Darling, let's run away tonight," she suggested, in the kind of voice you would use when ordering pizza, but like most things Octavia said, it felt like a command, not a suggestion. And like most of her commands, it sounded like it could get us in a whole lot of trouble. Naturally, I was more than up for it.

When we moored on Elephantine Island for our picnic, she took my hand and we made our escape. I paid another felucca some obscene amount of money to take us to the Old Cataract Hotel. I felt all cool and in charge as I negotiated the deal with the guy. Octavia seemed impressed too, which boosted my ego even more.

From a distance the hotel looked like a grand old palace hugging the bank of the Nile. It definitely called for the Leica, black-and-white film, slow shutter speed, and as wide an aperture setting as I could get away with. But I had the Hasselblad on me just as backup.

We got to the hotel expecting air-conditioning and luxury but armed guards shooed us away from the gates with their highly polished AK-47s.

Octavia laughed and swiped at their guns. "Darlings, don't be so silly," she told them, and like open sesame, the AK-47s were laid aside and the gates opened.

"I want to see the manager," she told the receptionist.

And tout de suite a haughty French dude with attitude to spare arrived. Octavia slipped her arm through his like they were old buddies and chattered away to him in French. Soon we were being ushered like royalty through the arabesque hallways and down onto the terrace where uniformed staff brought us apple shishas, mint tea, and Campari and sodas.

After we were left alone, Octavia casually suggested, "Why don't we stay the night? As tempting as the idea sounded, I knew it would create an international incident if Carol and Ms. Doyle noticed we were gone for even a minute, let alone the night.

"Isn't it gorgeous," Octavia cried, pointing at a brochure as I took some pictures of fellucas on the Nile. "Look Sam, look at all the lovely people who've stayed here. Tsar Nicholas the Second, Margaret Thatcher, Winston Churchill."

"Margaret Thatcher, lovely?"

"Darling, she did more for pussy bows and handbag politics than all the great fashionistas of the world put together."

"Handbag politics?"

"It's like voodoo economics. You have seen *Ferris Bueller's Day Off*, haven't you?"

"To handbag politics," I toasted. "Agatha Christie stayed here too," I pointed out. "Isn't this where *Death on the Nile* was set?"

"Yes, it says Agatha Christie stayed here while she wrote it. Oh Sam, we've *got* to stay. We can't miss an opportunity to spend a night in this monument to history. We owe it not just to ourselves but to our friends and family," she insisted.

I laughed. Octavia was the sort of girl you instinctively wanted to agree with—or rather, she was the sort of girl who made it impossible not to agree with her. Which is how we came to spend the night in the Agatha Christie suite.

CHAPTER 18

❤❤❤ OCTAVIA ❤❤❤

*One day when I'm three hundred years old and sailing
around the Med on my yacht with my teams of plastic
surgeons and life-support systems, I will regale
my nurses with this story.*

Sam was a darling but such a worrywart. Honestly, I wouldn't ever want to be caught in a really tricky situation with him. The poor thing had kittens when they demanded our passports in order to stay in the suite.

I realized that I would have to be the strong one, so I called Salah on his mobile and asked him to cover for us. Also, I told him we needed our passports for check-in.

"Octavia, the passports are in the safe," he told me, as if that should be the end of the matter.

But I didn't lose my patience with him. "Yes, but the boys at reception worship you like a demi-god," I reminded him. Sometimes boys miss the most vital signs. "Anyway, with Sam and me out of the way, you'll have no excuse *not* to pull Rosie."

"I don't know about that," he said.

"I know you think I haven't got a clue, Salah, but I know my friend better than you do. You've got to trust me."

He hesitated for a moment as if weighing what I'd said. Eventually he said, "I'll see what I can do," and then he hung up.

"You're friend is an absolute vacuum of joie de vivre," I told Sam after the call. He seemed very pleased that I'd said that.

"Are you sure you want to do this?" Sam asked when Salah called back to say he had managed to steal the passports and was sending them over.

"Anyway, we owe it to Salah and Rosie to give them some space," I said. I was only half-joking.

Sam nodded, then he pulled me in for a kiss and I knew he agreed.

It was all very Mata Hari–like, actually, and I knew it was going to be one of those memories you have forever. You know, the stories you go over and over in your mind and tell and retell until they become mythological in proportion. Only I didn't want to sound all sappy, so I said, "One day when I'm three hundred years old, as I sail around the Med on my yacht with my teams of plastic surgeons and life-support systems, I shall regale my nurses with this tale." Sam snaked his arm around my waist and started tickling me. I am still sure it was the best day of my life.

We rode up in an ancient etched-glass lift. The manager

was proud of it—it was all "restoration this" and "restoration that" and "famous him" and "famous her" and film, film, film—when all Sam and I wanted to do was lip-lock.

The suite was enormous and the first thing the manager did was open the wooden shutters to the balcony, offering up the Nile to us on an azure platter. It was glorious and in that moment I loved everyone: the hotel manager, even Nigel for forcing me to leave the Inner Zones. But especially Sam, who scooped me up in his arms and threw me onto the bed like a parcel of diamonds.

"Could you send up a bottle of Dom and a bowl of fruit?" Sam requested, handing over an unattractive bunch of crumpled bills. "We can take it from here."

I loved him being all manly like that, even if the effect was rather spoilt by the manager's lack of understanding of the American vernacular.

"Quoi?"

I translated Sam's request into French and the manager clicked his little French heels obediently. After he left Sam threw himself next to me and kissed me tenderly. To be perfectly honest, at that moment, my heart was pounding and I was feeling vulnerable, and a part of me wanted to say, "Only joking! Let's go back to the boat."

But after all that, I didn't even have the courage to run. And no, I wasn't worried that Sam was going to "take advantage of me" like some scoundrel from a Jane Austen novel. It was more serious than that.

I really, really, really liked Sam, and I knew he felt the same, and that was a place I'd never been before. A place where no one's in control or trying to prove anything.

So we stayed up talking all night, instead. Okay, there was quite a bit of kissing and cuddling, too, but that wasn't the Big Deal.

The Big Deal was that we told one another everything about each other. As dawn broke, Sam said, "You know, I think you might even know more about me than Salah does."

I kissed his forehead and snuggled into his chest. What I didn't tell him was the rather unsettling fact that I was pretty sure he knew more about me than even I knew about myself.

CHAPTER 19

♥♥♥ SALAH ♥♥♥

By midnight I finally touched the stars.

I called an emergency security council in Astin and Yo's room. It was almost six, which was when we were supposed to watch the video of our cruise. Yo was in the shower and Astin was on his BlackBerry playing a game. Rosie had run off to get Artimis and Perdie. If we were going to cover for Sam and Octavia, then we'd need all the help we could get.

"Sam and Octavia are spending the night at the Old Cataract in town and we're going to have to cover for them."

"Cool," Astin replied, slumping back on the bed without taking his eyes off the game.

Rosie arrived with the girls.

I watched as she sat neatly on the floor, in exactly the same position she'd been sitting the night I'd run my fingers through her hair. That seemed a long time ago now.

Yo came out of the bathroom, a towel around his waist, rubbing his wet hair with a bath towel.

"What's up?" he asked.

"Sam and Octavia are spending the night in that old hotel in town," Astin explained, still glued to his Black-Berry. "I'm just doing a search on it now. Here we go. Mmmm, nice crib. Hey, listen to this. Remember that DVD we watched the other night? The Agatha Christie lady wrote it there."

"She wrote the *book*, man. They didn't have DVDs back then," Yo told him, flicking his wet bath towel at Astin's head.

Astin snatched a wet towel from the floor and flicked it back at him.

"The real issue here is that if Nigel or Mr. Bell finds out about this, Octavia will be expelled," Perdie pointed out, grabbing the towel from Yo and chucking it back in the bathroom.

Artimis squealed, "And then we'll all be grounded or sent back."

"Okay, nobody panic. This is the plan," I told them. "We have to keep up the illusion that Octavia and Sam are on the boat. Like if anyone asks where they are, say something along the lines of, 'Oh yeah, I just saw them going out onto the deck.' That sort of thing."

"And we could call out to them as well," Artimis

said. "You know, like if we're leaving a room, we could call out to Octavia to hurry up."

"Or say she's on the phone," added Perdie, redoing one of her braids.

"Shame tonight's not a galabia party, then we could all dress up in disguises," Rosie offered. "You know, wear those fake mustaches. I've always fancied myself in one," she remarked idly. "But a really neat, groomed one, like Poirot's in *Death on the Nile*."

I loved that she said stuff like that.

"Actually, that's not a bad idea," Yo threw in. "Why don't we make it our own galabia party. You get all the girls to wear their galabias from the other night, with mustaches, and we'll wear . . ."

"There's no way I'm wearing a belly dancer's outfit," Astin said, looking up from his phone for the first time.

"Yeah, let's not do costumes," Yo agreed.

Astin—or any of us for that matter—in a belly dance outfit? "Yeah, let's not," we all agreed.

. . .

That evening, Nigel was wearing his safari suit and had his hair gelled flat. Carol was in a see-through cheesecloth kaftan looking up at him adoringly. It was kind of cute, really. The teachers insisted the Bowers Boys and Queens Girls sit on opposite sides of the room, which gave a sense of déjà vu—reminding us of that first awkward day on the *Nefertiti*.

"Right, well. We've all had a jolly nice time on this cruise," Nigel began, reading from speech notes as Rosie entered the room and took a place with her friends. Even from that distance I imagined I could smell her perfume—a sort of musk that reminded me of the markets of my childhood.

"I think we've all appreciated the cultural aspects of this trip, and not just of Egypt. I, for one, have found getting to know our friends from across the pond a most pleasurable experience."

Of course he meant Carol. Yo, Astin, and I whooped and whistled. That set the jocks off and everyone started clapping.

Nigel smiled and waved his hand to quiet us down. "Now, the cruise isn't over yet, but the crew have kindly taken the time to record some of our more memorable moments so that we might have a small memento to take back home. So without further ado, let's settle back and enjoy the show." Nigel chuckled. "Oh, and if you'd like to purchase a copy, they're available in the shop for twenty-five Egyptian pounds."

The lights dimmed and Arabic music pounded through the bar as the first images came up on the screen—starting with the girls getting of the bus with their luggage and walking up the gangplank to the *Nefertiti*. Rosie was wearing a white shift dress that showed her endlessly long legs; her strawberry-blond tresses were hanging down her back. I sighed.

Next, there was the shot of our school arriving and shouting to the girls on deck like the bunch of total jerks we were.

There were additional images of us coming and going from various sight-seeing trips. We all laughed at Mohammed stumbling around the temple complex at the Valley of the Kings and Queens wearing Yo's VR visor. There were shots of the girls looking hot in bikinis. Then came footage of the night I rescued Octavia from the other cruise boat. I froze as the video zoomed in on the Kiss. It really didn't look good. All the guys went nuts and I turned bright red. All I could think of as I watched myself lift Octavia into my arms was how it must have looked to Sam. And to Rosie. To make matters worse, the camera panned away before you could see the bit where I pulled away from Octavia's kiss.

I felt ashamed at how I'd treated Sam. No wonder he'd been pissed at me. I could have cleared it up with him and, more importantly, with Rosie, but I hadn't. I'd just arrogantly expected that Sam would trust me. I turned to make eye contact with Rosie, afraid that she'd be angry with me, but instead she smiled.

I still felt like a prize jerk.

By then everyone was laughing at the teachers dancing with the "Nubians" and Mr. Bell threw himself in front of the video screen. "Right, well I think that will be quite enough of that now!"

But everyone yelled for him to get out of the way, and Carol told him not to be a spoil sport. Mr. Bell marched over to the bar and poured himself a large whiskey.

The next bit of footage was a brief scene of Rosie, alone, playing the piano at night.

I'd never seen her play, I realized.

The next montage was one of Sam carrying Octavia on his back in the pool, followed by a long shot of Yo kissing Perdie, Astin fooling around with Artimis, and Carol and Nigel dirty dancing. No one was likely to forget *that* particular image in a hurry.

Everyone cracked up when the film revealed all four teachers in a conga line—at dawn. Nigel was wearing someone's bra over his polyester safari suit. Then it switched to a montage of each of the couples kissing each other, Sam taking pictures of Octavia, and then another montage of Rosie looking at me, me looking at Rosie, both of us pretending not to be looking at each other. Seeing it frame after frame made it all so obvious, and yet we'd both been totally oblivious of one another's feelings at the time.

I looked over at Rosie, who was blushing like crazy, and I thought, what the hell. It was a now-or-never moment and I'd wasted too many of those "never" moments on this cruise. So I did something so unlike me the entire room went silent. I walked through the seated crowds and stood in front of her.

"I really love the poem—" she began, but I didn't let her finish. Throwing fate to the wind I kissed her in front of everyone. A huge cheer went up from the jock brigade. But I didn't care and I don't think Rosie did either because she kissed me right back. When the lights came on, she sprung off me like a cat. My heart felt like it was going to pump itself out of my chest.

"Right, well, dinner now I think," Nigel said stiffly. "No dilly-dallying. By the way, where's Octavia, Rosie? I haven't seen her this evening."

Great, I finally get a real chance to kiss Rosie and the teachers notice Octavia's absence. I wanted to put my head in my hands and weep.

"Octavia?" Rosie repeated, playing for time.

"She's got a stomach thing, I think, sir," Astin told Nigel.

"Well, perhaps Carol should go down and see her."

"Oh, I wouldn't do that," Rosie warned. "She's sleeping."

"I might just go down anyway and make sure she's keeping her fluids up," Carol insisted, standing up.

"That's okay, I'll take it. She can get very snappy when she's sick," Rosie explained.

"That's true," Artimis added. "She, she, erm, throws things. She had our nurse in hospital for months when she came to school with a tummy bug once."

Carol looked at Nigel nervously. "All right, Rosie,

you go and make sure she's keeping her fluids up," she finally said.

Rosie stood to leave. "And maybe I'll go and check on Sam," Carol added. Is he in as well?"

"No," Yo jumped in quickly. "He was just here a second ago. He went to change."

"Yes, we've all decided to wear our galabias tonight," Astin added, thinking on his feet.

"Oh," Carol said. "Well, that's very ethnically embracing of you."

"Yes, erm, jolly good chaps," Nigel agreed.

We somehow made it through dinner without any more questions about Sam or Octavia.

After dinner the dance started. I took Rosie's hand in mine and led her out onto the deck. Underneath the canopy of the stars, she snuggled under my arm for warmth and I kissed her lightly on the lips.

"You still haven't let me thank you properly for the sheet music and the poem. I never really—"

But I kissed her then, and even though it wasn't the first time we'd kissed, it felt like the first *real* time. We were still kissing when Mohammed came out on deck. Rosie pulled away. "I'm, erm, that is, I'm going to check on Octavia," she said as she ran off.

I wanted to run off after her but Mohammed sat down next to me and said in Arabic, "I sometimes think these cruises are not Egypt. Not really. But other times like this I think this is very much my country, with all its history, the Nile, it stays constant. The source of all life."

Maybe it was because we were talking in Arabic that I confided my feelings for Rosie to him. I explained to him how she composed and how I'd never felt this way about a girl before and how I wanted to do something spectacular to mark our time together as it was going to be so short. Mohammed was a very soulful guy. He told me about how he had "wooed his wife."

"You know, my friend," he said, switching to English. "You need to make the grand gesture. The Egyptian heart is full of the romance of a great nation. Rosie plays the piano and we have on this boat the grand piano."

"True."

"Yes, true, in the bar. Use these oaf boys of yours to carry it out here under the stars so she can play to the fishermen of the Nile. This will mean more to her than diamonds and show her the fullness of your heart, my friend."

The "oafs," who'd been sneaking drinks from the bar, and were looking for ways to burn off steam, jumped at the suggestion to push the piano out on deck. They thought we were going to throw it into the Nile. By the time they got it outside, a chant of "Overboard! Overboard! Overboard!" went up. And sure enough, soon they began to lift it toward the railings.

"Hey dudes, why not throw Nigel overboard? instead" I suggested, only half-joking.

"Dude! That's brilliant," they cried, and chanted, "Nigel! Nigel! Nigel!"

Nigel was duly dragged from the dance floor with a concerned Carol in tow. Kicking and wailing, he was unceremoniously tossed over the side of the boat. I couldn't believe what I was seeing!

Carol screamed, "Nigel!" and dived in after him before anyone could stop her.

The reception staff and some of the other crewmembers looked down into the dark waters of the Nile where Nigel and Carol were flailing about and calling for help. Eventually the captain himself joined the crowd.

"This is not good," said the captain. "I think the police will be called. No, this is not good. These are bad people," he said, pointing to our floating teachers.

"No," agreed Mohammed. "This is not good. I am thinking they will be accused of buying hashish."

Rosie had turned up by that stage and was concerned. "Why will they be accused of buying hashish, Mohammed?" she asked. "They've been chucked in the water. Can't we get a felucca to fish them out or something?"

"We can, Allah willing," Mohammed agreed. "But still, I think the police will take them. Tourists buying hashish is taken very seriously in Egypt. We are not liberal about such things as the West."

"But they are so clearly not buying hashish," Rosie pleaded. "They're drowning. You've got to do something, Mohammed."

"See?" He pointed as a police speedboat charged toward Carol and Nigel. "It is as I feared," he said darkly. "They have been caught red-handed."

CHAPTER 20

··· ROSIE ···

Later, I would wonder if I'd have even done it had Octavia been there, or had I not been in Egypt . . .

There was a mad rush down to reception. Phone calls were made. There was lots of excited talk in Arabic and finally Mohammed confirmed that Carol and Nigel had been charged with drug smuggling.

"Honestly," I said, "have you ever met two more useless people in your life, Mohammed? I mean, have you seen Nigel's knees? Can you really believe they're capable of drug smuggling?"

"That Nigel is a hot head and disrespectful to the girls in his charge," he insisted, which as far as he was concerned rendered Nigel capable of anything.

Mr. Bell and Ms. Doyle went off to the police station along with the boat's captain. I didn't hold out much hope in the persuasive abilities of the teachers. If anything, having a man in a straw hat with a water bottle sticking out of the crown and a woman in camo could only make things worse. The captain had seemed as convinced of Nigel's guilt as Mohammed. With the boat now classified as an Authority-Free Zone, a cry went up to party and everyone tore upstairs to the bar.

Nigel might be an idiot but I still felt awful imagining him and Carol rotting away in an Egyptian jail. So I pleaded and groveled and cried until eventually Mohammed agreed to "do what he could" about getting the charges dropped on the condition I perform one of my compositions.

My legs went a bit soggy at first. I had never performed in the true sense of the word. I was a composer, not a performer, and never planned to play to real audiences. Audiences were Octavia's forte, not mine. I played for my music teacher and examination boards and various friends had heard me play, but I was so not a performer.

Mohammed was holding his hand out though. "Deal?" he asked. So I shook hands, reasonably confident that my promise wouldn't become a reality. For a start, the piano was in the bar, where the party was in full swing. Ha, ha, ha.

Only it wasn't.

The bar was empty.

Mohammed led me outside to the deck. The piano

had been moved outside under the stars. There were candles everywhere, flickering in the still night. I looked at the scene before me. Salah was standing beside the piano. It would have been a beautiful scene were it not for the fact that absolutely everybody else, from staff to students, was sitting cross-legged on the deck and looking at me expectantly. I turned to Mohammed. He grinned with pride. I froze with embarrassment. They expected me to play to an audience? Oh no.

Salah pulled the seat out and opened my composition. It was only because my knees were buckling with fear that I managed to sit.

Mohammed introduced me and during the whistles, cheering, and applause, I somehow managed to compose myself. I've heard it said that if you imagine your audience naked, it kills your nerves, but it's not true. From habit more than anything, I held out a trembling hand to touch my music. It was the score I'd been scratching away at since I got to Egypt, illuminated now by a line of fairy lights.

But I didn't need to see the score to know it because the piece wasn't something I'd learned. It had come through me. It had come through Egypt and the Nile and my muddled heart and my madder-than-mad mixed-up feelings for Salah. This composition was who I was in that moment and as I ran my hands lightly across the keys, I closed my eyes, fell into myself, and began to play.

The notes tingled down my arms and through my fingers. Slowly, as I lost all sense of where I was, my fingers moved with greater authority over the keys. I opened my eyes and looked up at the stars. It was an amazing feeling, actually performing in front of an audience.

I was so pumped with adrenaline by the time I finished that I didn't even realize how mental the cheering was. Deep down I suspected the rapturous applause was due to the drunken exuberance of the crowd rather than my own talent, but I loved every minute just the same. I'd never performed in public before and honestly, I never imagined that I would.

Later, I wondered if I'd have played if Octavia had been there, or if I hadn't been in Egypt, or if I'd ever perform again. But I wasn't analyzing it then. I was enjoying the moment. I wrapped my arms around Salah. I was just so glad he had made it happen. It was a perfect gift and I really wanted to say something deservedly monumental but words, as ever, failed me, so I kissed him and whispered, "Thank you."

. . .

I awoke as the sun was coming up over the Nile, my hair tangled about my face, my head on Salah's chest. It took a while to get my bearings because we were under the grand piano, which up until last night had been in the bar.

Salah woke up and kissed me. I was certain that my

breath must be gross as I hadn't cleaned my teeth, but he tasted like rose water. I had fed him rose water–flavored Turkish delight last night before we fell asleep, and he still had the sugar dust on his nose. I licked it off.

After breakfast, Carol and Nigel arrived in a disheveled state, moaning about police heavy handedness and the rampant injustice and corruption of power.

"And I'll tell you something for free, Carol, I'll be damned if those police weren't the same ruffians who arrested us at Edfu," Nigel whined.

"Nigel, I really think you're being paranoid. Edfu is a long way away from Aswan. Why would they come all the way here to arrest us when they didn't even know we'd be trying to buy hashish?"

"For the last time, WE WERE NOT TRYING TO BUY HASHISH, WOMAN!" he railed. Then he muttered something about Octavia being behind the whole thing.

"Where is Octavia, anyway? I wouldn't put this whole prank business past her."

Carol glared at him. "Oh, how typical of you to blame a teenage girl. I think you need anger-management therapy, Nigel, and in the meantime I'm going to take a shower and then go to bed!" With that she stomped off.

All was not well in their garden of love.

Later, Mohammed, Mr. Bell, and Ms. Doyle escorted us into Aswan. Mohammed took us to a slipper shop and then to a pancake shop and finally suggested we might all like some free time before rejoining the boat for lunch.

Salah and I had already texted Sam and arranged to pick them up outside their hotel, where a long line of caleches were gathered.

Octavia was stroking one of the horses while Sam nibbled her ear.

"Darlings!" she cried, throwing her arms around Salah and me. "We almost died from missing-you pains," she said, giving me a cuddle.

"So, we really got away with it?" Sam asked Salah, giving him one of those odd little American handshakes.

"Thanks to Nigel and Carol, who were arrested for trying to buy hashish." said Salah.

"Cool. I never took Carol for a hash fiend," Sam said.

"Can we take a caleche back to the boat, Sam, darling?" Octavia begged, jumping up and down.

The drivers all looked on with cartoon dollar signs popping out of their eyes. At that stage there was a lineup of over thirty carriages and no prospect of customers. Some of the horses looked pretty thin and weary. I felt sad for a couple of poor little skinny ones that didn't even have nosebags. The drivers were calling out to us in every language you can name, cajoling and joking, trying to engage us.

Salah started to talk to one of the guys in Arabic,

which drummed up a lot of interest from all the other drivers.

"Oh Rosie, the hotel was divine," Octavia said, linking her arm through mine. "We had the most amazing view. It was so unbelievably romantic. I never knew the sort of boy that makes you laugh can make you swoon as well." Sam nibbled her ear and gave me a grateful sort of look. Salah started to point at us as he spoke to the caleche drivers.

"Let's go see what Salah is up to," Octavia insisted.

"What's happing, man?" Sam asked.

"I'm trying to see how much they will charge us to let us race up the Corniche."

"Excellent!" Sam said.

Octavia jumped up and down on the spot while I went off to get some water, which I gave to some of the sadder ponies.

"So how much?" Octavia asked, as the men talked rapidly among themselves.

"They haven't agreed to do it yet," Salah admitted, looking a bit hopeless about it all.

Octavia spoke to one of them in her special persuasive way and then turned to us and said they'd do it for two hundred pounds Egyptian, with Sam's watch as deposit in case anything happened to their horses or carriages, or we get arrested.

"How did you get them to agree to that?"

"I pointed out that they had no other business and that Sam's watch would pay for an entire stable of fresh horses. Also I mentioned that if they were fast enough they could probably have it copied and sell it and he'd never know the difference."

Salah was suitably impressed. I realized it was the first time I'd seen him look on Octavia with anything other than irritation.

Then Sam and Salah wandered down the line of horses to choose their mount. Salah did some last-minute haggling in Arabic while Octavia and I climbed into the carriages.

"Okay, so we'll each take a driver for commands but we get to take the reins," Salah explained. "The winner gets to keep Sam's watch."

"Yeah, not wanting to be a party pooper here, but how did my watch even get involved in this?" Sam asked, clearly troubled as he looked lovingly at his watch. "My father gave me that for my bar mitzvah."

"No he didn't, you bought it for yourself last Christmas. I was with you," Salah said.

"All right! Winner takes the watch and don't spare the horses!" Sam agreed, climbing onto the driver's seat. He handed over his watch to the caleche owner who wasted no time in fastening the Breitling to his own wrist. "I suppose it's better than one of my cameras," he conceded cheerfully.

The Corniche was a large avenue that hugged the Nile. There wasn't much traffic on the road but what traffic there was, was really, really slow. I began to wonder if this was such a good idea, but we shot off so quickly I didn't have time to argue.

I was behind Salah, who was yelling his commands in Arabic. His co-driver was yelling with him. Sam was yelling too, and his driver was standing upright beside him screaming, "Breitling! Breitling! Breitling!" He was holding his watch up to the crowds of onlookers who swarmed along the Corniche. Aswan came out in force. Woman in black drapery, men in white galabias and turbans, shop owners, children, old people, and market owners with their chickens and donkeys all lined the street to cheer. Some of them took up the cheer of "Breitling!" The women made this amazing shrill sound with their tongues. Everyone was acting like they were at a Grand Prix. I'd never experienced such a rush of adrenaline. I don't know what came over me but I started screaming "Go, go, go!"

We raced the best part of a mile with our caleche inches ahead most of the way until just at the last turn when the roar of the crowd's of "Breitling!" deafened even Sam's decibel-breaking cries of triumph.

It was totally amazing. Sam hugged his driver. Salah hugged his. But best of all Salah hugged me. Octavia jumped over to my carriage and hugged me and then we were all hugging one another. Mohammed, who must have been watching the race from the boat, rushed down to meet us, climbed onto the carriage, and hugged us all.

"Now you are true Egyptians!" he told us, and for some reason this seemed liked the best thing anyone had ever said to us. "Completely, crazy, bloody Egyptians!"

Of course even though he'd won, Sam still gave his co-driver the Breitling. It would have been un-Egyptian not to, as Octavia said later on.

Saturday, Day 6
Nefertiti docked at Aswan

Sunrise: 06:26 Sunset: 17:58
5:00 Wake-up call
5:30–6:00 Breakfast in the Nefertiti restaurant
6:10 Pick up for bus to airport and flight to Abu Simbel
12:00 Return flight to Aswan
13:00 Lunch in the Nefertiti restaurant
19:30 Dinner in the Nefertiti restaurant
Sail to Luxor for return flights Sunday

CHAPTER 21

··· SAM ···

*My love is unique—no-one can rival her, for she is the
most beautiful woman alive. Just by passing,
she has stolen away my heart.*

The next morning we flew to Abu Simbel an hour
before dawn. Carol and Nigel came to breakfast but
told us they were returning to bed since they were still
recovering from their ordeal. They were not in the greatest mood. Octavia was wearing a tight orange T-shirt
with a cartoon factory from which little boys were
being manufactured. It read:

STUPID FACTORY WHERE BOYS ARE MADE

I cracked up with laughter.

Nigel told her to take it off as we were boarding the
bus to the airport, and she'd complied sweetly, exposing
her pink bikini top.

"That is not what I meant, miss, and well you know
it!" Nigel snapped. "Cover yourself up at once."

"This very bad man that he tells you to undress," Mohammed railed afterward. Later, on the bus to the airport, he was still working himself up about Nigel. "He is undignified and dishonorable. I do not like this man. Asking a young girl to undress is not proper." He was still going on about Nigel at the airport. None of us took much notice.

We touched down at Abu Simbel at 6:40 and hit the monuments ten minutes later. On the bus, Mohammed gave us his trademark blah, blah, blah about what we would be seeing at the site, but I couldn't concentrate. Octavia was resting her head on my shoulder and I was drugged on the whole smell and feel of her. She'd slept the whole way through the flight and it had hit me that tomorrow we'd be saying good-bye to each other and flying back to New York and London.

It seemed impossible that I had known her only a week and that after tomorrow I might never see her again. And I'm not even the sentimental sort of guy. A week is the shelf life of any relationship I've ever had, so why was I feeling so shortchanged?

The tourists who'd arrived for the sunrise were wandering up from the monuments as we walked down the dusty path. We were the only group on the streets that led to the monuments to Rameses II.

I stroked my hand across Octavia's cheek. Everything about her was so exotic. She was everything the ski-slope-nosed-blondes I normally dated were not. I decided then that Salah had a point; maybe they were pumped out on an Upper East Side factory line. Octavia was unique in every way.

As we walked past the souvenir shops that lined the path to Abu Simbel, Octavia suddenly grabbed my hand and pulled my thumb back teasingly until I fell to my knees in mock pain. All the storeowners came out and laughed.

"Buy something, darling," she said. "The shop owners look so forlorn."

"What do you want?" I asked, eyeing up the tourist crap displayed outside every shop. "You can have whatever you want from these Ali Baba caves. Name your jewels," I insisted, gesturing expansively at the bric-a-brac.

"I think you should get that stick that turns into a stool in case I want to sit down," she suggested, and so I bought four so Salah and Rosie could join us.

I was so glad I did because when we finally reached the monuments on the banks of Lake Nassar, we parked ourselves on them and soaked up the scene—along with the water in our bottles. In front of us was an aqua lake, behind us, the enormous pink edifice dedicated to Rameses II and his wife Nefertari. The walls of the temple were covered with images of Rameses smiting his enemies.

Mohammed left the others and joined us. Since our chariot race, we'd become his favorites. He pointed at the 167-foot-high figures carved in the rock.

"Imagine what the traders and invaders from Africa thought when they sailed up the Nile and saw this wall," Mohammed mused.

"Terror?" I suggested. "There's a lot of violence depicted."

"Yes. They would have been terrified of the kingdom they were entering and afraid of the mighty power of this great king. In the words of a great Englishman, they would crap their trousers."

Salah and I spat our water with laughter.

"Yes, but darling, who's that lovely woman with him?" Octavia asked.

"That his first wife. The most beautiful woman of Egypt ever lived. She very good woman. Very kind, very beautiful, very powerful and great. Rameses love her. She gave him sons. There is a poem we see in Luxor about her. Rameses II call her, the One for Whom the Sun Shines." That perked me up.

"Darling, I thought that was me," Octavia teased.

"Darling, it is you," Mohammed humored her. "The sun, it only shines for Octavia."

"There is a poem Rameses wrote for Nefertari," Mohammad said, and he recited the poem in Arabic. Salah was about to translate but I threw him a warning look. Salah smiled knowingly. I might not speak Arabic but I was pretty sure it was still sappy and totally the sort of thing I would want to say to Octavia. I was determined to get that and give it to her. Unlike Salah, writing poetry wasn't my thing.

"What does it mean in English?" Octavia asked.

"Ahh," Mohammed said, reading my pleading look. "That would be telling, Octavia. Even a bright girl like you can't know everything."

"You are the wisest tour guide any of us could have wished for, Mohammed," she said.

After that, we went into the temple complex itself, where men in turbans and galabias guarded giant ankh keys to open the chambers. They, in turn, were guarded by soldiers with AK-47s. Salah gave them some baksheesh on Mohammed's instructions so that we could go into some of the secret chambers tourists weren't allowed into. Mohammed told us stories about this great Pharaoh who had ruled over Egypt for most of his ninety-six years of life. He explained the triumphs of his battles in Syria, which were depicted in detail on the walls.

"Darling, he was mad keen on winning wars, wasn't he?" Octavia remarked.

Mohammed laughed. "Yes, darling, he was mad keen."

When we returned into the blazing desert sun, Mr. Bell was giving his own talk to the others. "It is a magnificent monument to a venerated leader of the ancient Egyptians and with the pink desert contrasted spectacularly with the azure blue of the lake, it makes a most impressive spectacle. More impressive than the Pyramids of Giza, according to many." Hearing this short guy with a water bottle stuck in the crown of his straw hat, crapping on about magnificence, made us all crack up.

I spent the next ten minutes taking shots of the monument. I got a fantastic one of the soldiers with the gatekeeper and more shots of their boots and the butts of AK-47s in the sand.

Soon our small group wandered off alone again into another temple. I don't think I was the only one in a pensive mood. It was hard not to focus on the fact that tomorrow we would all be going back to our real lives. As if reading my mind, I got an e-mail from my dad confirming he'd pick me up at JFK Airport.

The next temple we entered was full of couples fooling around in the semidarkness, which Mohammed wasn't too happy about. He used his stick to chase them out, saying they were being disrespectful of the temple. I was no better, though, because on the way back I ended up selling my iPod for the same price I'd paid for it in New York to the guy we'd bought the stools from. Still, you only live once.

Back at the airport, Octavia turned to me. "I think we should buy Mohammed something to remember us by," Octavia suggested as we waited for our flight back to Aswan.

"I know," Salah said. "Let's get the shop to embroider 'blah, blah, blah' in hieroglyphs on a T-shirt."

"*Bloody* blah, blah, blah," Octavia corrected.

Once we were on the plane, I approached Mohammed and asked him to write out a copy of the poem he'd recited at Abu Simbel. It said:

> *My love is unique. No one can rival her, for she is the most beautiful girl alive. Just by passing, she has stolen my heart.*

Back at the boat, I copied it onto a postcard of the Great Sphinx and put it in a package that I planned to send to Octavia at her school in England. I added the sand I'd pocketed and the stone sphinx from the Valley of the Kings and Queens. On the bottom, I etched the answer to my riddle. I was hoping that it would be waiting for her back in London when she returned.

CHAPTER 22

❤❤❤ OCTAVIA ❤❤❤

It was tres, tres Romeo and Juliet on the Nile.

Nigel, you look ever so cross," I told him when we were back on the *Nefertiti*.

"Into the lobby! All of you! Now!" he roared.

Given we were already there, it all seemed a bit melodramatic, but then that's the way with teachers.

The staff nervously handed out the usual cold flannels and cups of ice water as Nigel and Carol stood silently to the side, waiting for the ritual to be dispensed with.

"Right. I want all of you to march up onto the deck in single file this very moment."

A few of the group obeyed wordlessly, but most ignored his suggestion and began to make our way to our cabins.

It was about then that Carol screamed, "Do what Nigel says!"

"Yes! On the deck now. That's an order!" barked Nigel.

"What's this all about, Nigel?" Mr. Bell asked after his ears had stopped ringing.

"You'll see soon enough," Nigel warned darkly.

When we had all filed out onto the deck, Nigel was standing by the piano, which for some reason was out there. Everyone was listening while he ranted, with all the hand movements of a general. When people lose their sense of proportion, I find it best to give them space. In Nigel's case, I suspected it might take some time before he regained his composure, so I grabbed a towel and quietly slid myself onto a sun lounger at the back.

I didn't have a clue what he was talking about. Sam looked at me and shrugged. Rosie gave me a warning look and shook her head, but I wasn't to be deterred from my task of sun worship on our last day in Egypt.

"And what do you think you're up to, madam?" Nigel demanded of me as I settled on my towel. "Come here this instant and stand here with the rest of the group."

Carol was calmer. She explained, "Yes, Octavia, this is very important. You see, Nigel and I were both too tired after our ordeal with the police yesterday to come upstairs until just before you came back. And instead of relaxing in the sun, we discovered this, a piano out here!

The captain says that it's been damaged, and we're not leaving until the guilty party confesses to how it got out here."

"Well, as I wasn't even—" I was about to say "on the boat" but luckily Sam cut me off with a look.

"—capable of moving a piano. So, it couldn't possibly have been Octavia." Sam added before I shot off my mouth about spending the night with him at the hotel in town.

"Exactly," I agreed gratefully.

"Will no one own up to what happened to the piano?" Carol asked. Her question was met with silence.

"In that case," said Nigel, "I have decided to put you all under cruise arrest. That means that apart from lunch, dinner, and breakfast tomorrow, you will all be locked in your cabins until we depart for our respective flights."

I always knew that Nigel was a funny little man, but at that moment, I feared he might be seriously certifiable.

"Darling, I'm sure all that arrest business was most unsettling, but if you play in the mud and buy drugs, you have to expect to get dirty," I said playfully. "Mohammed explained that buying hashish is a very serious crime in Egypt."

"For the last time, I did not play in the mud!" Nigel blustered. "I was manhandled over the side of the boat by hooligans." He had begun to foam at the mouth and it was hard to resist an urge to take a tissue to him.

Mohammed entered the discussion. "Nigel, I have warned you the buying of hashish in our country is a serious matter. When in Egypt you should do as the Egyptian do and act respectably," he explained.

"I think Mohammed has a fearfully good point. You should try and be more Egyptian and respectful of others," I said.

Sam came over and stood beside me and put his finger to my lips. "This is our last night—let's not rile the teachers."

American boys really do worry too much. I turned to him and kissed him lightly on the mouth. That was when Carol blew her whistle.

"Right, missy! That's it. Into your cabin! Now! You can have your meals in your room. You will be released not a moment before the bus to the airport tomorrow morning."

Sam turned on her. "Carol! You can't do that! This is our last night together."

"Yes, and you're not my teacher anyway!" I added.

"Don't you tell me what I can and can't do, young man," she yelled deafening the entire populace of the Nile. It is shameful the way teachers have such a lack of respect for other people's pleasure. And anyhow, how dare she speak to my boyfriend like that.

"I don't want to have to call the police and have you arrested again, Carol," I warned her, but my teasing was muffled by Rosie, who put her hand over my mouth to shut me up. "Quiet, Octavia! Seriously, do you want to get us all grounded? This is our last night!"

Unfortunately, Rosie's reasoning was too late to save me from myself. "Right, that's it!" Nigel exploded. "I've had enough of your impertinence. I said get down to your cabin! And I mean. NOW!" he roared.

I felt awful. Sam, Salah, and all the others began pleading with the teachers. I closed my eyes and put my hands over my ears and listened to the drumbeat of guilt in my head. Maybe Ferris Bueller was wrong—what if you could go too far?

Suddenly I felt my sun lounger being lifted. I looked down. I was being carried through the bar and downstairs to my room by the bar staff. It's true that I felt just like Cleopatra, which I enjoyed. But my pleasure was short lived as I heard the awful sound of the key locking my door from the outside. My freedom was over.

After watching a bit of television, I had the bright idea of e-mailing the staff on my BlackBerry. I asked them to call the police on Nigel for imprisoning me, which amused them greatly. But seriously, I couldn't find much to be happy about. I watched miserably as we moved out of Aswan and began sailing back to Luxor. I wondered what Sam was doing. He probably hated me now.

Later, Carol turned up with a tray of lunch and was very sweet.

"I'm sorry about all this. I know it's your last night and if you ask me, Nigel's gone a little bit overboard. I think he just feels he owes it to your parents to discipline you."

Sensing her weakness I tried to work on her. "Papa and Mumsy will die when they hear I was locked in a cabin on a cruise."

I felt I'd rattled her a bit because she put down the tray on my desk, sat on Rosie's bed, and looked into her hands. "He is being a bit dictatorial," she conceded.

"A bit! He's Mussolini! That's what we call him at school," I lied.

I could see she was concerned now because she was biting her lip, and I began to hope. I don't think Carol was a big fan of fascist girl-imprisoners. "Eat your lunch and maybe he'll allow you up for dinner," she suggested. Then she left me and locked the door. It was awful.

Rosie joined me about an hour later. By then the hatefulness of my situation really hit me and I started to cry. This cruise-arrest business meant that Sam and I wouldn't be able to have any time together ever, ever, ever again.

Rosie was crying too. We held one another and sobbed about the injustice of it all as the banks of the Nile slipped passed. Then Sam texted me, and Salah texted her, and then we realized there was an actual phone in our room. They're called land lines.

You know those old-fashioned ones with cords that you used to see in films? Anyway, we used them to call the boys in their room because that was free. They were as shocked as we were to discover how romantic cord phones are. You can cradle them against your neck while you lie in bed and the signal is beyond wonderful.

Salah even called the boat's gift shop and managed to arrange for Mohammed's hieroglyphic BLOODY BLAH, BLAH, BLAH T-shirt to be printed. Perhaps he wasn't such a grump after all, I told Rosie. "No one could accuse him of being a selfish boy, when in a time of great hardship and distress he is able to think of others." The gift shop assured Salah that the T-shirt would be ready for collection that evening before dinner.

Rosie and I tried to get the most out of our solitary confinement by showering, doing our hair and nails and chatting to Salah and Sam for the next few hours until we were eventually released for dinner. But, even then, the boys had to sit on one side of the room and the girls on the other.

I point-blank refused to accept this hideously evil and hypocritical ruling when all the teachers were happily mingling with the opposite gender. I made a point of sitting down beside Sam.

Rosie followed suit and seated herself by Salah, and a

mass rebellion of reseating began to take place, with Nigel going la-la and Carol trying to reason with us. Both were ignored and Mohammed warned Nigel that his behavior was not acceptable in Egypt, a land that could trace a sophisticated civilization back thousands of years. That put Nigel in his place.

Hateful, hateful, hateful Nigel.

"Darling, I can't bear this," I told Sam as our starters were brought in.

"Have mine," he offered, switching plates. He is the dearest, daftest boy in all the world and I gave him a kiss on the cheek.

"I meant this being our last night," I explained.

"I know you did," he replied with a smile, then gave me an Eskimo kiss.

Rosie giggled and Salah held her hand. We had to grab our happiness where we could. It was all very Romeo and Juliet on the Nile.

"Sam and I have a plan," Salah told us, leaning back in his seat.

"Be at your window at nine o'clock," Sam whispered into my ear. Honestly, boys are like cryptic crosswords.

I didn't get to unravel what on earth he meant because that was when Ahmed brought in the T-shirt we'd ordered.

"I think you should do the honors," Salah told me, which made me feel, I don't know. Special?

I stood on my chair and called for quiet.

"I'd like to make a toast to a great man!" I began, tapping my glass with a fork.

Everyone stopped eating and chatting—apart from Nigel, who had an apoplectic fit and told me to get down or he'd send me to my room without any supper. Carol told him to shush.

Anyway, I ignored him. "We've only known Mohammed for a short time, but in that time he has taught us all about ancient Egypt and brought the gods and goddesses to life for us."

The jocks all started to cheer and a chorus of "Moham-med" went around the room and everyone stood on their chairs.

"Mohammed," I called above the growing din. "Please come to the podium—well, stand up on my chair anyway." I stood on the table.

He came over, his Indiana Jones hat proudly on his head as he sheepishly climbed onto my chair.

"We girls of Queens and boys of Bowers would like to present you with a memento of our affection." I held the T-shirt with the hieroglyphics on the front up to the crowd. Then I turned it around where the words BLOODY BLAH! BLAH! BLAH! were emblazoned in English and Arabic on the back. Everyone, especially the teachers, applauded. I thought Mr. Bell and the others would break their hands with all their clapping. Ms. Doyle even blew her whistle and whooped!

Mohammed put the T-shirt on over his other shirt and touched his heart with his hand and gave us a little bow.

Nigel then made his own speech and said he was very proud that we students had got so much out of our trip. But not proud enough to release us from prison apparently, because the next thing we knew, we were headed back to our cabins for lockdown.

CHAPTER 23

··❤ SALAH ❤··

*Sam was right. Egypt was totally crazy! And I finally saw why
he loved crazy. Because with crazy, magic happens.*

I'd hatched a plan to see Rosie while I was lying in bed,
pissed off with Nigel and Carol. This was our last
night! I kind of felt responsible for the cabin arrest as
it was me who'd organized moving the piano onto the
deck and I should have been the one to have it put back
where it belonged.

Still, I can't deny that sneaking out under the cloak of
darkness to see my girl appealed to the poet in me—or
was it the ancient romance of my Egyptian soul?

I'd shared my plan with Sam that afternoon.

While we'd been moored in Kom Ombo earlier in the
evening, I made a deal with a local fisherman named
Siad who agreed to ferry me and Sam from our cabin
over to the girls' rooms on the other side of the boat.

Mohammed had agreed to position himself at a local café to keep an eye out for Nigel. "Don't you worry, I will take care of him!" he'd assured me.

Siad picked Sam and me up at the prearranged time. We climbed out the window, into the felucca. So far our plan was going smoothly. "This is like James Bond stuff, man!" Sam joked. But I was crossing my fingers because when it came down to it, there were too many things that could go wrong if we messed up.

The girls' room was on the bank side of the Nile, so Siad helped us tie ropes around our waists and lowered from the bank to the deck where their cabin was.

I was the first to scuttle down the bank but Siad's grip wasn't exactly what you'd call professional, and instead of landing Bond-style at the girls' window, I was dunked headfirst into the Nile. By the time Siad managed to haul me level to the girls' window, I had swallowed a few gallons of Nile water. "No problem, my friend. This is good luck for you," Siad assured me. "Drinking the Nile means you will always return."

"Yeah, for his funeral," Sam told him.

And then it got worse. Instead of finding the window open as I'd requested in my text message, the window was firmly shut and the girls were curled up in bed watching television. This left me, face pressed against their windowpane, feeling like a dead insect on a windshield. I banged on the glass.

Eventually I got their attention. "Hello," Octavia said, opening the window. "What on earth are you doing here of all places? You look like a drowned rat."

"We told you to open the window at nine," I reminded her.

"Oh. We thought it was like a cryptic spy-thriller thing."

"What?"

"You know, the eagle flies at dawn, that sort of thing," she explained as she mimed speaking into an earpiece.

"So, can I come in?" I asked, plucking something soggy and lumpen—I didn't even want to imagine what—out of my ear. Rosie pulled me into the room.

After Sam made his slightly drier journey down to the cabin, I gave Mohammed the all-clear and tied a bundle of notes to the rope for Siad. I figured I'd probably set him and his family up for life. And it was worth it to be with Rosie.

Even though we could only glimpse the stars and we had to share the room with Sam and Octavia, that night definitely goes down as one of the most romantic of my life. If anything, Sam and Octavia being there enhanced, things. Somehow, the bizarre confusion of our getting together made it all the more magical.

With Rosie tucked under my arm. I had never felt more in love or more Egyptian. I even told her I loved her in Arabic, and she repeated it back to me. Her British accent made it all the more adorable because like English, every Arab-speaking country has its own accent.

We stayed up all night, talking and kissing and reminiscing. None of us spoke about how tomorrow we'd be flying home, or even whether we'd see each other again. Around dawn, we fell asleep for an hour before the call for breakfast. That was when the agony of parting really hit us.

The farewells on the boat were formal. The staff all lined up to shake our hands.

Mohammed came up to me. "Salah, you must always remember, it is noble to speak your heart, but it is not always necessary to speak your mind."

We kissed cheeks and hugged. I know it was kind of pathetic but Mohammed had pretty much summed up how I felt about life. People say a lot of things they really don't need to. All the crazy stuff that had gone down between all of us on that cruise was pretty much a case of not saying what was in our hearts. Instead we'd played too many crazy head games.

. . .

We were all traveling together to the airport, but for a change hardly anyone spoke.

Carol had bought Nigel a gold ankh from the souvenir shop on the boat and he'd undone several buttons to show it off, but not even that could make us laugh. A dark mood had descended on all of us.

Our flight left later so we were in line with the girls when Nigel got all worked up about being seated at the back of the plane. Apparently he and Mr. Bell had paid for first class. Mr. Bell, who had no problem with his seat just said, "Bad luck, old man."

Nigel insisted he wasn't going to take it lying down! His tantrum attracted a group of police.

I could have stepped in and had a word with the police but the way I looked at it, Nigel kind of had it coming. So instead I took the opportunity to kiss Rosie one last time and pretty much everyone did the same.

I found it interesting that Carol pretended to be immersed in a search for her passport as he was led away, yelling about "Bloody Egyptians!"

"You can do better," I whispered to her as the police led Nigel away, their automatic weapons aimed squarely at his shorty shorts. But I think at that stage, she knew that already.

. . .

As we stowed our trays for takeoff, I thought back to when we'd arrived and my fears that my guys wouldn't get Egypt. Sam turned to me, slapped me on the back, and said, "*Magic country,*" and I felt almost choked because I knew then that Sam totally got Egypt, which meant in a nutshell, he got me.

All the guys said pretty much the same thing. They totally got the crazy magic of Egypt. So I guess what I'm saying is, this hadn't been just another school trip, all about hot foreign girls and partying.

Not that there wasn't plenty of that too.

CHAPTER 24

••• ROSIE •••

Coda: A passage of more or less independent character introduced after the completion of the essential parts of a movement, so as to form a more definite and satisfactory conclusion. Oxford English Dictionary

When we arrived back at school the next day, there was a package with a card and some items from the Valley of the Kings and Queens waiting for Octavia from Sam. On the card was the love poem to Nefertari that Mohammed had recited in Abu Simbel.

Nigel returned to school a week later. Only there was no more talk about us calling him Nigel, anymore—he was back to being Mr. Menzies with us again. But that didn't matter because we were all calling him Shorty Shorts behind his back anyway. It was business as usual in geogers that first day. He handed out the work sheets we'd have to do about our trip.

"Right, girls! The fun and games are behind us now. It's down to real work. Exams are coming up and this trip will be an important part of your marks. I'll expect these work sheets back by the end of the week," he informed us.

At the top of the sheet was the riddle of the Sphinx. Only not the one Sam had given Octavia.

What walks on four legs in the morning, two in the afternoon, and three in the evening?

We all asked what it meant.

"Think girls, think! Humankind," he said with a sigh after we threw out a few useless suggestions. "Think about it. A child crawls, an adult walks, and a senior walks with the aid of a stick. I thought it rather pertinent for all of us after our journey to the land of the pharaohs. We all grow and change with experience. I think it is true that all of us were changed immeasurably by our experiences in Egypt."

"Well, I much preferred Sam's riddle," Octavia whispered, turning over her sphinx to reveal his riddle and the answer, which he had scratched into the base.

Q: What creature has two hearts?
A: Octavia, for she has stolen mine away.

I smiled even though I was a bit jealous (some things never change). I hadn't heard from Salah since we parted at the airport.

But wishes do come true because a postcard from Salah arrived a few days later. It was a postcard of Abu Simbel he'd bought in Egypt. After that, I received one every week, each one depicting one of the monuments we'd visited on our journey of riddles and misunderstandings. It is three months now and we are still e-mailing, texting, and calling. He's coming to London in the summer with his father to have his suits made.

Artimis and Perdie have other boyfriends now, but Octavia has kept up communication with Sam and she always has the sphinx he gave her on her desk at school.

Out of all of us she's been changed by Egypt the most. I mean, she's still Octavia and madly over the top, but she's dropped a lot of her crazy act. Like the Inner London thing—thank goodness.

Or like the day we got home from Egypt, when she told me that her crumbling ruin of a house is literally falling apart and that her family is penniless.

I said, "Who cares? You are still titled and fabulous and at least you don't have a materialistic hypocrite for a father and a house full of horrible brothers who tease you all the time."

"True! Papa is a darling," Octavia said. "Actually, Sam said pretty much the same thing—not about brothers and materialistic hypocrites but the who cares part. So, do you want to come and help me give the tours this summer?"

I think I might. They have an "awesome" harpsichord I can play, and Octavia thinks the tour groups will love my atmospheric music. I think I'll enjoy the audience. Salah has totally ruined computer composing for me—those programs just don't do justice to the music in my head the way an audience can. It's strange, but even though he's so far away, every thought I have is filtered through him now. And while I can't see the stars in the London night sky, I still look up and think of him. Once really, really late at night, he sent me a text.

I thought I saw Osiris in the sky but it was just a bunch of planes circling overhead. It reminded me of you, S x

ACKNOWLEDGMENTS

Egypt rocks in every way. The people, the history, and the customs all combined to work their magic on me so much so that I lived there for almost three years. Going back to research this book made me wonder what on earth possessed me to leave. Nothing beats sailing down the Nile for romance, but doing it with a bestie—my magnificent friend Katia Sergeeva—turned it into a party. Every day on *Alexander the Great* was like being the birthday girl. Our Egyptologist, Mohammed, was a scholar and a gentleman.

Inspiration is all well and good, but every author dreams of the vision and talent of editors like Melanie Cecka and Stacy Cantor at Bloomsbury USA. Special thanks also to Laura Dail of the Laura Dail Literary Agency.

As ever, shout-outs go to my family and friends but especially to my daughter, Cordelia, and son, Zad, for enduring, with grace, the horrendous existence of being children of an author.